CYBERCLIPPER

JASON O'NEIL

authorHOUSE®

AuthorHouse™
1663 Liberty Drive
Bloomington, IN 47403
www.authorhouse.com
Phone: 1 (800) 839-8640

Published by AuthorHouse 04/21/2017

ISBN: 978-1-5246-8874-5 (sc)
ISBN: 978-1-5246-8876-9 (hc)
ISBN: 978-1-5246-8875-2 (e)

Library of Congress Control Number: 2017906067

Print information available on the last page.

This book is printed on acid-free paper.

Contents

Cast of Characters

Prince Omar Khalid
Member, UAE Royal Family
Age: 41
MBA, London School of Economics
Cigarette boat racing enthusiast
Palace in Dubai
Looks Like: Omar Shariff, actor

Ms. Dahlia Samira
Prince Khalid's personal assistant
Age: 30
BS in Computer Science, Cambridge University
Loves all water sports
Looks Like: Carla Ossa, supermodel

Prince Yousif Latif
Member, Dubai's High Society
Lifetime friend of Prince Khalid
Age: 40
PhD, Mathematics, UCLA
Avid polo player with a string of ponies
Looks Like: Young Pablo Picasso

Tom "Catfish" Crowley
Senior Megayacht Captain
Age: 55
Aeronautical engineer turned sea captain
Lives in Hamilton, Bermuda
Looks Like: Ernest Hemmingway, Author

Anthony "Tony" Caselli
Supertanker Captain
Age: 48
BS U.S. Naval Academy, Nautical Engineering
Looks Like: Joe DiMaggio, Baseball Hall of Famer

Tanner Jolie
Captain, Carnival Cruise Lines
Age: 50
Nautical Engineer; Power plant specialist
Cigarette boat racer in Miami, Florida
Looks Like: Robert Redford, actor

Dr. Adam Raviv
Israeli computer whiz; Inventor of GSMem technology
Age: 36
B.S. Tel Aviv University, Computer Science
Likes water sports
Looks Like: Young Einstein

Amy Grossberg
Computer Scientist; Cyber Specialist
BS; Summa Cum Laude, Tel Aviv University
Age: 30
Kung Fu Black Belt; Fitness Model
Looks Like: Shlomit Malka; Israeli Fashion Model

Amira Atara
Computer Scientist
M.S.; Columbia University; NYC
Age: 34
Lead Engineer in Computer Security Firm
Consultant to the Banking Industry
Hobby: Global Trekker
Looks Like: Natalie Portman, actress

Tom van der Heyden
Communications Engineer; Wireless guru
Age: 32
B.S. Temple University, engineering
Family man with 5 children
Looks Like: Young John Glenn, astronaut

Ann Nichols
Retired Banker; Tour Guide in San Francisco
Age: 55
Married Tom Crowley's brother
MBA, University of Southern California
Looks Like: Lauren Bacall, actress

Audrey Goldman
Retired Linguistics Teacher; Tour Guide in New York City
Age: 49
MS, Linguistics, Yashiva University
Godmother to Adam Raviv
Looks Like: Older Esti Ginsburg; Israeli Supermodel

Monika Strassberg
Austrian Countess; Ski Instructor
Age 38
Tall, striking blonde
Looks Like: Maria Sharapova, tennis player

Win Parker
Harbormaster, Bermuda
Age: 50
Member, Britain's America's Cup Racing Team
Avid sport fisherman
Looks Like: George Clooney, actor

Ben Myles
Computer Operator; Software Analyst
Age: 45
MS, Cyber Security, Fresno State University
Motorcycle enthusiast; mechanic
Looks Like: Marlin Brando, actor

Nigel Stark
Senior Detective, Interpol, Lyon, France
Age: 60
BA; King's College, Cambridge
Leader: Sherlock Holmes Society in London
Looks Like: Basil Rathbone, actor

Foster York
INCAT Plant Manager; Hobart Australia
Age: 50
MS, Maritime Engineering, Adelaide University
Considered a hull design genius
Avid Sailor
Looks Like: Young Michael Caine, actor

Dominique Villefranche (Nikki)
Magayacht saleswoman in Monaco
Age: 36
Bikini Model
Looks Like: Dominique McElligott, actress

Bruce St. John
IBM Supercomputer salesman; Blue Gene Model expert
African American
Age: 42
MS, Computer Science; Carnegie Mellon University
Looks Like: Sidney Portier, actor

Katie Flynn
Marina Manager; Cabo San Lucas, Mexico
Age: 32
Sailed solo from Mexico to Indonesia; Makes fitness videos
Looks Like: Kathryn Budig; Fitness Instructor

Nathan Kalish
Porsche salesman in Redondo Beach, California
Age: 39
Trusted friend of Prince Latif from UCLA
Looks Like: Steve McQueen, actor, race car driver

Steven Goldberg
Retired Stockbroker in NYC
Age: 49
Husband of Audrey Goldman
Trusted friend of Prince Latif
Looks Like: Steven Segal, actor

Jacques Malreau
Audi car test driver
Age: 34
Based in Nice, France
Looks Like: Mario Andretti, race car driver, in his prime

1

FORMATION

Prince Omar Khalid, a member of the UAE Royal Family, has put out a call for a meeting in June at the Oberoi Hotel at 1 Bay Street in downtown Dubai City. The Prince has been involved with megayachts (over 200 feet long) all his life. He is an avid cigarette boat racer and loves speed on the water. At age 41, he has applied his MBA from the London School of Economics to accumulate a vast fortune. He has helped develop Dubai's Maritime City and megaport. He is part owner of the Oberoi Hotel and other new buildings in Dubai.

Much to the chagrin of other members of the Royal Family, the Prince remains a bachelor and is usually seen in public with his assistant, Dahlia Samira. Only age 30, Ms. Samira has the reputation as a 'hot shot" computer scientist with a degree from Cambridge University north of London, England. The former Miss Dubai and swimsuit model, she serves as a Project Manager for the Prince.

Prince Khalid's confidant, indeed, right-hand man is Prince Yousif Latif. Prince Latif is a life-long friend of Prince Khalid and at age 40 is frequently seen in Dubai's High Society. The Prince earned his PhD in mathematics from UCLA. He's an avid polo player with several strings of ponies. He is a shrewd negotiator and buyer on behalf of Prince Khalid. His dark, piercing eyes remind one of Pablo Picasso.

Today, the trio is in Prince Khalid's suite on the 26th floor of the hotel awaiting three individuals who will be instrumental in executing one of the Prince's bold undertakings. The first person to arrive is Tom "Catfish" Crowley. The 55 year-old megayacht captain with 30 years of experience on the high seas was trained as an aeronautical engineer but turned into a maritime sea captain. People in his home port of Hamilton, Bermuda often say he looks like Earnest Hemingway. As his taxi pulled up to the hotel, Dahlia was in the cool black and white marble lobby to greet and escort the Captain up to the Prince's suite.

As the elevator door opened into the suite with its dramatic 180 degree view of the new megacity, Prince Latif approached the Captain with an outstretched hand of greeting. Prince Latif was the first to speak: "Captain Crowley your reputation proceeds you. What an honor to meet you."

The Captain, or Skipper as he is sometimes called by peers, replied: "Thank you, Your Highness, it is truly a pleasure to be here." "And, Captain, I have the pleasure of presenting His Highness Prince Khalid," said Prince Latif. As they shook hands, the Captain bowed his head in respect. The Prince also warmly welcomed the seasoned voyager. He then motioned the Captain to be seated at a long ebony conference table and enjoy a cup of tea.

Only five minutes later the elevator doors opened revealing Dahlia and a short, rotund man dressed in khaki slacks and a black Hawaiian shirt with large yellow Hibiscus blossoms. Prince Latif approached the man saying: "Tom van der Heyden, I presume." "Yes, Your Highness, that would be me at your service," replied the gentleman. The 32 year-old communications engineer known as a "wireless guru" with many publications in print, then said: "I don't know how you found me on a remote island, but here I am and eager to learn about your project, Sir." Tom took a seat at the table. Van der Heyden scanned the room intently as though he was searching for listening devices or "Bugs."

No sooner had van der Heyden taken a sip of his tea when the elevator doors opened. Dahlia motioned for the guest to step into the suite as she said: "Your Highnesses, please meet Adam Raviv. The 36 year-old Israeli computer whiz was warmly welcomed by the Princes and introduced to Crowley and van der Heyden. Van der Heyden immediately had a flashback of a young Einstein. Prince Latif introduced the inventor of many cyber sleuth technologies by saying: "Computers are not secure when Dr. Raviv is involved. He is the inventor of GSMen technology which you will learn about later."

It was quickly revealed that everyone at the table had a love for the ocean, even Raviv who raced on jet-skies and did blue water fishing to unwind from professional tension.

Prince Latif opened the meeting by saying: "You are our guests for the weekend. You will learn of our project and enjoy Dubian hospitality. But first in order for you to do so, you must sign the Non-Disclosure and Pledge of Secrecy which Dahlia is placing in front of you." Each of the guests was given a Montblanc Meisterstuck pen to sign the document. All three forms were signed, and the Prince said: "Very well. And you may keep the pen." Smiles broke out around the room. The Prince continued: "Your visit will consist of two major briefings and opportunities to see our modern metropolis. You will also please me to be my guest for dinner at my residence," said Prince Khalid. The guests nodded their approval. "And if you're really quick learners, we'll have time to go out on my go-fast boat," joked His Highness. The strangers—soon to be a cohesive team- all laughed with a nod of approval.

"Each of you has a vital role to play in our project, indeed, adventure. But let me warn you that there will be some danger in what we do. However, the reward will be huge. And you will each share in it," stated Prince Latif. He continued: "You are free to go now, but once you are briefed, you're committed. Is that clear?" Nobody got up from the table.

"Very good," said the Host. "You will now be briefed by Prince Latif on the first element of the project. Yousif, please proceed." Dahlia turned on a laptop and closed the blinds at the end of the table to form a movie screen. Soon the screen was lit by a video showing a revolutionary trimaran megacraft. The 300 foot long boat was shown in a variety of configurations such as a car ferry, disaster-relief supply vessel and military applications including tanks and troop landings.

Captain Crowley was quick to speak up: "I know that craft. It's a High Speed Craft (HSC) made down under in Hobart Australia."

"Exactly, Skipper. You're right," said Prince Latif. "It's made by a company called INCAT in Hobart, Tasmania, an island state off the south coast of Australia. There are about one hundred of them around the world serving difference purposes. America bought two for military demonstration purposes. Prince Khalid toured one of them last year when it visited our Maritime City. You can tell by the man standing on the dock in this view, that it is huge, 310 feet long and 88 feet wide. And as shown in the data package in front of you, it is very, very fast. One of its secrets is that the middle trimaran rides above the water and creates lift rather than drag."

"Captain Crowley. What do you think? Would you like to pilot one of these beasts?" asked the Prince. "It's quite different than the cruise ships."

"It would be an honor, Your Highness," replied the Skipper. "Will it be a ferry boat here in the Middle East?" inquired the Captain.

"No, far from it, my new-found friend," replied the Prince. "You'll learn about its use during your stay here," replied His Highness. "And you're going to love its home ports!"

"Ports?" asked Captain Crowley. "Did you mean plural, several ports?" asked the Captain.

"I sure did," replied the Prince. "You see, one will be based at your home port of Bermuda. But there will also be one in Cabo San Lucas and one in Monaco. You see, we'll be buying three HSC's in order to complete our mission, provided you and two other skippers are convinced it is the right craft for our project," continued the Prince. "But, Captain Crowley, you and you alone will know the exact nature of our mission. The other two skippers will perform their duties without a need to know the ship's real purpose. Do you understand, sir?"

"Yes, Sir. I do!" replied the senior seaman.

"Fine." "Now let's go over some of the details of this megayacht," continued Prince Latif. But before we do, I want to make it perfectly clear that you Mr. van der Heyden and you, Dr. Raviv, must know every feature about this craft as though you own it. You will not be piloting it, but your role in our project requires you to understand this technology platform in great detail in order to perform what will be asked of you. Is that clear, gentlemen?" asked the Prince.

The two men looked at each other and said in unison: "Yes, Sir!"

For the next one and one-half hours, the INCAT documents were examined. Different configurations were each analyzed. Captain Crowley was particularly interested in the weight and balance calculations as well as the propulsion from the water jets. He examined some of the reliability statistics of the key subsystems. The group was impressed by the quality of the nautical-based questions and comments by the Israeli…maybe he is an Einstein. At noon, lunch was brought into the suite as the team continued to learn about the HSC and each other.

Promptly at 2:00 PM Prince Latif said: "Gentlemen, it's time for a break. Our car is waiting to take you on a tour of the new Maritime City, complete with covered wharfs where our HSC's will be re-fitted for the mission." Ten minutes later a Mercedes-Benz Maybach entered the wharf area. The Prince gave a walk-around briefing of the facilities and their capabilities. It was clear that he had played a vital role in the design, development and commissioning of this world-class drydock for the construction and retrofitting of megayachts, typically over 250 feet in length. The work force appeared to be primarily for the Far East and were housed in tall, modern apartment buildings, complete with retail and entertainment complexes. At 3:30 the three visitors were asked to return to the Maybach. Ten minutes later, the limo pulled up to the entrance of the Dubai Gold Souk. Each of the visitors was handed an envelope which contained $10,000 in Dirhum to be spent in the Souk.

"Please accept this as a token of our appreciation for your participation in our project," said the Prince. "Now go and enjoy the next hour as you pick out something for yourself or a loved one. The car will return at 4:30 to take you back to the Oberoi. You will have 2 hours to relax, perhaps visit the spa and dress for dinner. Proper outfits are already in your rooms. At 6:30 our car will leave for Prince Khalid's residence for dinner and a question and answer session."

By 6:30 the trio was getting used to enjoying the Maybach. This time the Mercedes-Benz drove to the suburb of Al Karama near the Palace of the Sheikh Ahmed. As the gates to the residence opened, a building in the likeness of a French chateau appeared before their eyes. The trio, now dressed in fine, white silk tunics, climbed the front steps. As they entered the building, one metal covered everything: gold. His Highness Prince Khalid descended a spiral staircase to greet his guests. He joked: "Did you buy anything for me at the Souk?" Everybody laughed. Tom van der Heyden thought to himself: "Now, I know how a King lives."

As the Princes led the party into the bar area, they were met by Dahlia who wore are stunning gold and black dress ready to serve an adult beverage. During cocktails, the Host detailed some of his accomplishments in the development of Dubai. He also gave great credit to his friend, Prince Latif, for his ability to create iron-clad, enforceable contracts with on-time delivery clauses and stiff penalties for default.

"Too bad you can't stay a week," said His Highness, "because Latif will field his polo team in a critical match. But you will already be busy with project tasks, I assure you, if I know my friend the Prince," said Prince Khalid.

Dinner was a sumptuous, extravagant affair. Each course was better than the previous one. Dr. Raviv was used to pottery dishes and stainless steel utensils back in Tel Aviv. He took some personal reflection before he put the gold fork to his lips. Captain Crowley has given up smoking many years ago. But he couldn't resist the Prince's offer of a fine Cuban cigar and a cognac after dinner. In the conversation each guest revealed a little more about himself. Tom van der Heyden, the communications expert, seemed to appreciate the rationale of why this particular trio came together...but for what purpose?

The Host ended the evening by saying: "Tomorrow you will be briefed twice—once in the morning and once in the afternoon. You'll have two hours free time, but one hour will be taken up by a VIP visit to the Burj Khalifa, the tallest building in the world. Somehow a cocktail tastes differently, 124 stories above the Earth. Then tomorrow evening it will be Prince Latif's pleasure to entertain you. I don't think you'll be disappointed," ended the Prince as bid his guests farewell. The Maybach knew the way back to the Oberoi.

At 9:00 AM the trio entered the Prince's suite. Strong, black coffee awaited them. Again, Dahlia powered on a laptop for a slide show.

Prince Latif started the meeting by asking a question, "Do you know what a Blue Gene is? That's B-L-U-E G-E-N-E as he spelled it out.

"Of course," said Dr. Raviv, "it's one of IBM's supercomputers, one of the most powerful, yet efficient, in the world."

"Correct, Doctor, said Prince Latif. "You're absolutely right." The BLUE is for IBM and the GENE is for project to map the genome.

"Here are several slides that depict the computer," continued the Prince, as he narrated each one with details that impressed his guests. The uses for such computer power are varied and usually are carried out by research institutes trying to solve difficult problems." The Prince continued, "To give you an idea of the Model "L's" computer power, the machine's 131,000 processors routinely handle 280 trillion operations per second."

"Yes, and I bet the data streams are so large that multiple, parallel networks must be employed," said van der Heyden.

"Absolutely, right, Tom." "Opps, may I call you "Tom?" asked the Prince.

"Of course, Sir," replied the communications expert.

"Ok, enough of this "Sir" stuff; we're a team now. And first names are no offense," replied the Prince with much authority in his voice.

It was at this point when the Skipper made a key point: "But you don't need a supercomputer to run a HSC."

"Captain, you're absolutely right," replied the Prince. "As you know there are thousands of small computers and sensor systems on a cruise ship, but altogether they don't equate to the compute power of a Blue Gene L," replied Yousif.

At this point, Dr. Raviv broke into the conversation by saying that "supercomputers are routinely used by the military in missile defense applications and by the Intelligence Community to foil computer intrusions and/or conduct offensive operations against other systems. Indeed, they can even crack encryption codes."

"Right you are, Doctor, "replied the Host.

"I may be a bid dense, but I still don't see how or why a megayacht and a supercomputer come together," stated the Skipper in an inquiring tone.

"Captain, we're going to spend a little more time discussing the Blue Gene before we break for our skyscraper tour," said the Prince. "It will all come together this afternoon. I assure you, sir."

On the trip back from the el Burj Khalifa, a lightbulb went off in the seaman's cranium—a megayacht with a supercomputer close enough to shore might be used to clandestinely crack a computer's encryption scheme. And the data would be there for the taking. As they pulled up to the Oberoi Hotel, Tom noticed a slight, almost devilish, smile on Adam's face.

2

INCAT

Aboard Prince Latif's Gulfstream V business jet over the Pacific Ocean, the inspection/evaluation team of Dahlia, Captain Crowley and Captains Tony Caselli and Tanner Jolie were briefed by the Prince about the purpose of their trip.

"We'll refuel in Tokyo and then proceed past Sydney to the southern-most part of Australia. We'll land at Hobart, the capital and most populous city of the Australian island of Tasmania," said the Prince. "Founded in 1803 as a penal colony, the city now supports a growing number of expeditions to Antarctica."

"It's harbor is the second-deepest natural port in the world," continued the Prince.

"We'll be there three days as we inspect one of the most revolutionary sea craft ever devised, the INSAT High Speed Craft (HSC)," said the Prince. Prince Khalid toured the U.S. Navy's HSC, called 2 SWIFT, when it called on Dubai two years ago. Ever since then, the Prince has baselined this megayacht for the mission. By this time tomorrow you'll understand why."

Captain Crowley then spoke up: "I've seen videos of the sea trails. It's huge and yet very fast."

"You're right, Skipper, replied the Prince. But it's even bigger in person. But it needs to be to accommodate our payload. Indeed, at 310 feet long, it will be ranked as the 41st largest megayacht on the planet. And we're in the market for three of them to be fitted out at our Maritime City in Dubai," said Prince Latif.

Seven hours later the Gulfstream landed at Hobart International Airport. The plane was met by a silver Maybach for the short trip to the central business district where it stopped at 38 Murray Street in front of Hobart's most famous and most opulent hotel, Hadley's Orient Hotel.

"We have eagerly awaited your arrival, Your Highness," said the woman at the front desk. The team was escorted to an ornate dining room filled with 19th century British furniture and a crystal chandelier in the middle of the room. It was 3:00 PM and Hadley's traditional Afternoon Tea Experience was enjoyed by a handful of tourists. The team was led to a round table in the corner where a tall, slender, very-distinguished gentleman stood up to greet the Prince and his party with a warm welcome.

"Welcome, Your Highness, I'm Foster York of INCAT. I will be your host and guide during your team's visit. And you can imagine based upon our email traffic, we're excited you're here," said Mr. York. After introductions all around the table, the guests were served a wide variety of scones and Danish pastries.

"It's a long flight, but we're rested and eager to learn about your very special sea craft," stated Prince Latif.

"Well it's special alright. And you'll see the shipyard is buzzing with activity. And as promised, you'll be treated to two demonstrations on the high seas," continued Mr. York.

"That's what we agreed to," replied the Prince. "And I've deliberately not provided too many details about the craft to my team so they can provide an unbiased evaluation."

Plant Manager York than took the liberty to set up his tablet on the edge of the table and narrated a sixty-minute slide deck about the HSC. The team seemed reticent to ask questions. Perhaps they were just in awe of the magnitude of the Prince's adventure.

That evening three other INCAT managers joined Mr. York to have a rack of lamb dinner at the Orient Hotel. All three were former megayacht captains who had been won over by the HSC and the Tasmanian lifestyle. Captain Crowley asked most of the questions, typically about the craft's handling characteristics in high sea states with waves typically six feet high.

The General Manager was quick to reply to each question with a simple, albeit sincere response: "They don't exist. The HSC rides above the waves and literally surfs above them at an incredible 52 miles per hour."

At 10:30 PM the party broke up with everyone looking forward to tomorrow.

After a seemingly never-ending breakfast buffet, the team assembled in the hotel lobby promptly at 8:30 as the Maybach appeared under the hotel's canopy. It was only a ten-minute ride to INCAT's shipyard in the Derwent River Park suburb of Hobart. The company's cavernous boatyard gleamed in the bright morning sunshine. A sign at the front gate blinked the number 88, the number of high speed catamarans INCAT had in service around the world, usually as ferries but some delivered for military logistics purposes.

Plant Manager York greeted the car and escorted the Prince and his team to a briefing room. The respective parties took their sides at the long mahogany conference table and each poured a second cup of coffee. Mr. York then introduced the design team responsible for the HSC. Over the next two hours, the engineers provided a complete description of the standard craft. Two videos showed the HSC in full operation, one as a ferry in Hong Kong and another as a military craft in Singapore. Latif's captains took copious notes on their tablets and laptops as they poured over the documents provided by INCAT. And just before lunch, the team was shown a confidential video showing the 2 SWIFT in its sea trails in the North Atlantic. Some "minor" superstructure damage was found, but there was no hull damage, even in sea state 8.

Dahlia was quick to finish her lunch and excused herself to have a quick cigarette on the cafeteria terrace. She reviewed her entries on her tablet:

- Wave-priercing, aluminum trimaran hull
- Modular design to be refitted to support missions without long shipyard periods
- No drag center hull
- Propulsion by directional water jets, so the ship has no propeller or rudder allowing maneuvers in as little as 12 feet of water
- Length: 321.5 feet
- Beam: 88.6 feet
- Draft: 11 feet
- Capacity: 600 tons
- Cargo Deck: 29,000 square feet
- Crew: 17 mariners
- Helicopter Flight Deck
- Waterjets: 4 Wartsila LIPS/LJ12OE which also allow a reverse function
- Decks: Cargo, Personnel and Bridge
- Communications Center, complete with multiple terrestrial and satellite systems
- Rear-loading deck and ramp for vehicles and watercraft
- Use as Ferry: 950 people; 250 cars

Dahlia finished her cigarette (she doesn't smoke in Dubai), shook her head in amazement and rejoined the group for the ride to the pier for the first demonstration.

The Maybach drove around the bay to the marina's test station. As the car pulled up to a bright yellow INCAT HSC bound for ferry service in the Philippines, the team was in awe of this mega-sea vehicle. Foster York approached the team and motioned for the Prince to lead the way up the gangplank. Some fifty steps later, the Prince was heartily greeted by the Test Team Lead.

"Your Highness, you're in for a real treat today, Sir," he said. "We'll be doing some speed trials in the form of figure 8's, and the 20 knot winds should put the vehicle to a real test."

"I wish to see the cargo bay first," said the Prince.

"Of course, Sir, right this way," was the right answer as the engineer led the team down a steep ladder to the cargo bay. Soon the team was standing in the middle of the 29,000 square feet cargo bay. Six lanes of cars could easily fit into the space. The Prince's eyes met those of Dahlia and Catfish with an unspoken satisfaction.

The ship's whistle blew, and the crew untethered the HSC from the dock as the team climbed up two ladders to the bridge. The captain greeted the team and asked them to have a seat on the leather bench behind the helm. As the First Mate piloted the new ship out of the harbor and into the Tasmanian Sea, the captain described the functions of most of the video screens above and below the 180 degree windshield.

The test team lead than gave the signal to the bridge to begin the prescribed maneuvers. It seemed only a few seconds before the massive craft was "flying" above the water at tremendous speed. As it made a graceful turn in the figure 8, the long white wake came into view.

Captain Caselli remarked, "Prince, this is remarkable, there is virtually no vibration."

"I know, Skipper," replied the Prince. "It's one of the primary reasons we're here."

The speed trial then called for a series of start, stop and restart the engines, and all of the activities were performed flawlessly.

During the second hour at sea, the Prince's team was given a briefing in the Information and Communications Center (ICC) directly behind the bridge. It was a glass-enclosed room about 20 feet by 20 feet filled with large displays and monitoring instruments. The test parameters—temperatures, pressures, fuel usage, cooling liquids and dozens of others were on display. The room was devoid of any red alarm signals. In short, all of the subsystems were passing the test.

After two and one-half hours on the ocean, the test team had all the requisite data and gave the signal to return to port. On the return trip, the Prince's evaluation team toured the crew deck and various rooms to be used by the ferry crew. The crew quarters were sparse but adequate. It was easy for the Prince and Dahlia to visualize the right layout for their mission. The right choice of materials, and the HSC could be turned into a luxury yacht, even one with a clandestine purpose, known only by a handful of people.

That evening INCAT sponsored a lobster dinner in the Prince's honor in the banquet room of the Orient Hotel. The Prince and General Manager anchored both ends of the long table seating twenty quests. The mayor of Hobart was also an honored quest. A multi-media lightshow about INSAT's products ran continuously at one end of the room. After dinner, the smoking lamp was lit, and sea stories were told on the verandah until midnight.

During the morning of the second day, the team visited the design studio for discussions about alternative configurations for outfitting the HSC as a luxury megayacht. Various interior decors were projected on video screens. Dahlia realized immediately how easy it was to spend megabucks in this domain.

After lunch at a seafood restaurant in the central business district of Hobart, the team was driven to the pier for the second demonstration sailing. This HSC was about to be delivered to a Russian oil tycoon who had outfitted with lavish staterooms, lounges, movie theater, swimming pool and gym and spa. Dahlia took hundreds of pictures for use back in Dubai.

For this demonstration test, the Prince asked his three sea captains to each focus on a particular area.

- -Capt. Crowley: Propulsion
- -Capt. Caselli: Electric Power Systems and back-up generators
- -Capt. Jolie: Navigation and Communications

As the HSC was executing the required tests, the Prince walked around the five-story behemoth deep in thought. He spent much of his time below in the cargo bay. He took measurements via a hand-held laser measuring device. He also inventoried the safety features of the craft, complete with tenders and inflatable Zodiacs suitable for crew evacuation.

During the in-bound leg of the test, he joined Captain Crowley in the ICC.

"Catfish," he asked. "Are the communications systems secure and redundant, indeed, fail-safe?"

"Yes, Sir, they are," answered the Skipper. "I've been impressed. The owner has spared no expense to have a very capable communications center."

"Very well," replied the Prince. "Please get the specifications so we can clone it in Dubai."

"Yes, Sir," replied the Skipper. "I've already requested the configuration drawings."

As the HSC slowed down to enter the harbor, the Prince asked his captains if they had all of the data they needed to make an informed decision(s), rationale for outfitting the three catamarans necessary for the mission. All of them answered in the affirmative via nodding heads. Captain Jolie stated that he was sure he could increase the speed by ten knots by tuning the engines and using an upgraded fuel.

"Excellent," responded the Prince. "But will we lose efficiency and cost us miles per gallon?" asked the Prince.

"No, Sir," was the reply. He continued: "We'll plan to purchase HSC's which already have the upgraded Catepillar engines."

The Prince liked what he heard. He then stepped out of the bridge onto the docking platform and sent a secure text message via satellite to a mansion in downtown Dubai with a cryptic note: "The platform is a go. Have the data and will return via Monaco."

The final farewell banquet was held in the Glass House restaurant, 5-star restaurant on a dedicated pier at Book Street on Franklin Wharf. INCAT reserved the entire restaurant and invited key supervisors as a thank-you party. The restaurant's fare was primarily Japanese, Asian and, of course, New Zealand lamb.

An HSC ice sculpture was flood-lighted in the middle of room ringed by a lavish buffet. Foster York toasted the Prince and the team. The Prince reciprocated by thanking his generous host and their "superior" watercraft. At the end of the dinner, General Manger York provided a list HSC's for sale around the world. He also pointed out key supervisors in the audience who would be available to perform re-fit work at the Dubai Maritime Terminal. This gesture was very well-received by Prince Latif.

The Maybach delivered the team to the aircraft at 8:30 the next morning. Handshakes and pats on the back provided a warm send-off for the Prince's team. Within twenty minutes, the Gulfstream was climbing along the eastern coast of Australia ready for the flight to Honolulu. For most of the flight, the captains huddled around a conference table comparing notes and swapping suggestions on how to configure an HSC to best meet the Prince's requirements. The Prince spent a lot of time on the telephone. They all knew with whom he was talking but didn't understand a word he was saying. During refueling in Hawaii, the Prince announced that the next destination would be the tiny country of Monaco. The team members didn't speak. They simply smiled as that rested their heads on the leather pillows. Dahlia and the captains knew that Monaco was a haven for yacht brokers, particularly for very large boats.

3

MONACO

During the morning of the next day, the Prince's jet touched down at the Nice Cote d'Azur International Airport which serves the principality of Monaco only 14 miles east on the coast of the Mediterranean Sea. The team was chauffeured to the Hotel de Paris Monte Carlo next to the famous Monte Carlo Casino. The doorman instantly recognized the Prince and welcomed him back. In the lobby, the evaluation team was directed to consolidate their findings over the next two days and provide a report by the end of the week. Dahlia's photos would supplement the engineering details provided by the Captains.

After freshening up in his suite, the Prince overlooked the harbor and spotted the yacht which was his destination. In crisp white Arab men's dress, complete with Ghutra, Igal, Bisht and Dishdasha, the Prince alone walked down hill on Avenue d'Ostende to the Quai Hirondelle pier at the Hercule Marine. After showing his credentials to harbor security, he walked confidently down the middle of the Quai to the megayacht, Dardanelle. Only moments later he stood on the bow spa area with his shadow covering a bikini-clad woman sunbathing by the pool.

"Excuse me, Sir, but you're blocking the sun!" she exclaimed. No sooner had she said the words, and she realized it was her friend Prince Latif.

"Your Highness, what a pleasant surprise!" "But I didn't expect you until this afternoon," said Dominique Villefranche, the 36 year-old French beauty who happened to be one of the world's foremost yacht brokers.

"You're absolutely right, Nikki, but my request is so unusual that I thought it best to come early to give you more time to search the planet for the items to meet my requirements," said Prince Latif.

"Oh, I see," said Ms. Villefranche as she took a seat at the poolside bar.

"You see, I've done my homework," continued the Prince. "You represent the company, Yachting Partners International (YPI), the London-based largest yacht broker in the world. I know you're one of their most successful salespeople. And I really need your help now."

"Well, sir, I've been very blessed, indeed very lucky," responded Nikki with some humility in her voice.

"Yes, both lucky and smart," continued the Prince. "You've flourished in a world typically dominated by "good 'ol boys," responded the Prince.

His Highness continued: "I think we can do some business together. Would you be kind enough to join me for lunch at the Hotel de Paris where I'll explain my requirements?"

"I'd be honored, Your Highness. I can be there at noon," replied Nikki.

"Perfect," replied the Prince. "In this way, you'll have the afternoon to research your client base and make some suggestions, perhaps by dinner time."

"Well, Your Highness, I know you as a man of action, responded Nikki with some real excitement in her voice. "I accept your gracious invitation and will do my very best to fulfill your needs."

The super saleswoman than stood up, held out her hand, gave a firm handshake followed by a slight bow of her head as she said," See you at noon, Prince."

"I look forward to it, and please call me "Yousif" if you're comfortable in doing so," answered the Prince as he walked over to the gangplank to leave the boat.

It was a beautiful, sunny day as the wealthy saleslady entered the lobby of the Hotel. The concierge immediately recognized her and said," How nice to see you Mademoiselle Villefranche."

"Likewise, Francois, always a pleasure to see you in one of my most favorite places on Earth," responded Nikki.

"Your party awaits you at the far end of the Café, actually at the very table you usually reserve," replied Francois.

"Perfect, I know the way," said Nikki as she turned toward the Café with a cute, almost sly, smile on her face.

As she approached the table…HER table…, the Prince stood up and extended his hand in friendship.

"Sir, I mean Yousif, how many people reject your invitation?" asked Nikki. They both laughed as she took her seat. The couple ordered Perrier water and surveyed the menu. Yousif started the conversation by saying, "Nikki, I bet you have this menu memorized. What do you recommend?

"Well, I usually get the escargot and the daily quiche," replied Nikki.

The order was placed, and the Prince pushed an envelope across the table to Nikki. The yacht broker scanned a couple sheets and exclaimed," Wow, your timing couldn't be better, Sir. I mean Yousif." "I'm very familiar with the INCAT products, and there are several on the market right now. Indeed, a couple ferry companied have just filed for bankruptcy, and you can really get a bargain. And I see you've done your homework because your short list is quite appropriate."

"Nikki, that's what my research shows. But I don't need "A" bargain. I need three of them!" responded Yousif with uncharacteristic volume in his voice.

"Three!" responded Nikki. "What are you going to do set up a ferry service in the UAE?"

"No," replied Yousif. "I need three to be re-fitted in Dubai for a very special mission."

"Yousif, these are huge vessels. You must have huge plans," responded Nikki with an inquiring tone in her voice hoping the Prince would divulge something about his mission.

The Arab was silent and only smiled slightly. It was clear to Nikki that this would be a HUGE sale, but she may never know the purpose for these megayachts. After lunch, the Prince and the broker parted at the Hotel's front door with a promise to meet for dinner to discuss some options and terms.

Nikki returned to the Dardanelle, logged onto the YPI database and within a couple minutes emphatically spoke out loud: "That's it! I've found the perfect one!" She then called her manager in London to report the news. Minutes later she got a call with two more suggested INCAT HSC's for her esteemed client.

As she dressed for dinner, she said to herself, "This is going to be a really big day. Heck, I might even end up at the casino."

For the second time in a day, Nikki entered the lobby of the Hotel de Paris Monte Carlo, this time dressed in a floor-length, silver sequined gown with a plunging neckline revealing a diamond necklace in her cleavage. Her hunch proved correct that her client was already seated at a corner table in the famous Louis XV restaurant with its guilded Baroque ambiance.

The Prince was all smiles as Nikki approached the table and simply said; "You look ravishing, indeed, exquisite, Nikki. Are you sure you want to talk business?"

As she sat down, she replied in a firm voice: "Of course. Business before pleasure, you know!"

"Of course," replied Yousif. "I hope your research was successful, my good broker."

"It sure was," exclaimed Nikki with a genuine excitement. "We are prepared to offer three HSC's at what the Americans call: "Bargain Basement Prices." "I will provide all of the details to you in the morning. But's here's some photos of the vessels," as she pulled a small envelope out of her black opera purse. As the Prince looked at the pictures, Nikki stated some of the terms to buy 3 HSC's—one each from France, England and Greece.

"You see, Yousif." "Your timing is perfect. These ferry companies can't even pay the insurance much less the mortgages on these craft. They have released most of the crews and are desperate to get them off their books," exhorted the broker who continued: "Indeed, you would be getting an $80M vessel for about $20M which includes our fee. I hope you can appreciate the value I propose."

The Prince raised his glass and clinked Niki's saying: "My friend, this is very exciting. We may just have a deal here. I will commission three survey teams to inspect them over the next two weeks. Indeed, I already have the Captains to lead the inspection teams. If the survey's prove out, I would expect you to have the contracts ready to negotiate in your YPI offices in Dubai within a week. Is that acceptable?"

"Of course," replied Nikki. "I can make that happen."

"Well then let's enjoy dinner, and perhaps you'll join me in the baccarat room in the Casino. I think you'll bring me good luck!" said Yousif.

"Yousif, I'd be honored. I'd love to," replied Nikki as she envisioned walking into the room with the Prince by her side.

It was almost midnight when the couple walked across the plaza from the Casino to the Hotel. As Nikki got into an awaiting limousine, Yousif said: "I was right. You brought me luck tonight… in more ways than one."

Without showing affection in public, he shook her hand and said: "Good night, Nikki, I really look forward to your visit to Dubai."

The next morning as the Prince's jet was climbing out of the Cote d'Azur, three Captains were dispatched to the HSC's to complete the surveys on schedule. Prince Khalid was pleased with the progress report.

4

ALMADEN

It was almost midnight when the Prince's Gulfstream landed at the Ben Gurion Airport serving Tel Aviv and taxied to the civil aviation hangar. As the plane was refueled, Prince Latif met Dr. Raviv and his assistant, Amira Atara in the Sky Lounge. Ms. Atara is a cyber security specialist who graduated summa cum laude from Columbia University in New York City. She is only 34 years old but already has an international reputation on how to keep banks and financial institutions secure. Dr. Raviv introduced Ms. Atara to the Prince and Dahlia.

An hour later the four-person party was headed west toward America. After an uneventful flight across the Atlantic Ocean, the jet landed at Dulles Airport just west of Washington, D.C. After the plane taxied to the Signature private aviation building, stopped and lowered the stairs, a young man with a small suitcase climbed into the airplane. As he entered, he was greeted by Dahlia who introduced Arne Lindquist, a distinguished computer scientist who is an expert in supercomputer operations. Once airborne, Dahlia served breakfast and the members of the party became more acquainted.

After a four and one-half hour flight, the jet landed in San Jose, California. The plane was met by a black limousine for the 18-mile ride south to the IBM Research Center in Almaden. Nestled in the rolling hills of this 700-acre preserve are four modern buildings housing about 500 engineers and scientists responsible for many of the company's next generation products. As the 5-person party signed in at the lobby, the display of computer disk drives held the party's interest.

Within minutes, the Center's Director, Dr. Tryg Ager, was greeting his guests and escorting them into a wood-paneled conference room. Preparing for a slide show, Dr. Bruce St. John, IBM's leading supercomputer salesman, walked over and introduced himself to the Prince and his party. Coffee was served and the lights dimmed as Dr. St. John proceeded to fill the next 2-hours with "petaflops of data" and videos about the Blue Gene Model L supercomputer at the Prince's request. Indeed, Dr. St. John was responding to a 3-page specification sheet provided in advance by Mr. Lindquist. When asked what the application for the machine, the Prince gave a vague answer about financial modelling.

At this point in the meeting, the Prince stated: "Let me make myself quite clear. I'm in the market for three Blue Gene's," as he held up three fingers to emphasize his point. "They are to be delivered to our Maritime City in Dubai within the next 5-months."

The room went silent as all eyes were on the IBMer.

Dr. St. John replied, "Well, Your Highness, it's probably possible since 2 of our clients are currently upgrading to the new model "Q", and you could procure them used but still under our warranty." Always the consummate salesman, the tall, striking African-American activated his tablet on the end of the conference table, pushed the F-7 key and displayed a list of installations which would be most appropriate.

He then continued: "The closest would be at the University of Brunei where the upgrade is almost complete. Indeed, some of the "L" racks are already in crates.

This pleased the Prince: "Excellent, and the other two?"

"Well, Your Highness, my recommendation would be the machine at the University of Nevada where their project about artificial neural networks just finished and also the Blue Gene L machine here where we are upgrading to the "Q" to demonstrate high speed analytics and artificial intelligence to a U.S. Government customer. Both of these could very well be delivered within your timeframe, but we would have to clear it with headquarters in Armonk first."

At this point, Dr. Ager added: "Dr. St. John has outlined a most reasonable and timely plan. I will commit to give you proposal within 2-weeks. But, Your Highness, please remember that these machines take 1.2 megawatts to operate. You would probably have to operate them at night or have a dedicated power supply."

"Thank you for the reminder, Doctor," responded Prince Latif. "I have a solution for that."

"And you'll want special cooling in the floor of your data center in order to disburse the heat from the 64-racks of equipment. "continued Dr. Ager.

"Sir," responded the Prince, "we have a design for that as well."

"Oh, and shipping will cost you at least $2M from here and Nevada, but probably only $1M from Brunei," added Dr. St. John. The rest of meeting focused on contractual details.

On the second day in Almaden, the Prince's team pelted the IBM engineers with questions before and after touring the Blue Gene L facility. Meanwhile, the Prince and Dahlia had excused themselves and visited friends in Portola Valley, just south of San Francisco. One of the friends was Nathan Kalish, a trusted friend of the Prince's from his days at UCLA.

At the end of the day, Dr. Raviv called the Prince to inform him of the team's findings and that they were prepared to return to Israel.

"Very well," replied the Prince. "We'll depart from San Jose at 9:00 PM tonight."

Three weeks after the Almaden visit, Dahlia had finished her review of the IBM sales contract, made some minor clause changes and suggested that the Prince wire 30% of the contract value as a down payment until the three computers arrived safely in the Maritime City's air-conditioned warehouse, all 200 wooden crates, costing over $100M for which only a handful of people knew the application.

5

THE DEALS

On a clear, sunny May morning, Nikki was enjoying breakfast after a workout in the gym on her beloved Dardanelle yacht when she got the call that the last of the 3 HSC's had successfully passed the survey inspections and sea trials to be eligible for insurance by Lloyds of London. By mid-afternoon she had finalized the terms of the sales to be presented to the Prince for approval and final payment in Dubai. At the same time, each of the captains and their First Mates were interviewing potential crew members. It took a month for all of the credentials and background checks to be complete and two weeks of familiarization cruises before the catamarans departed for Dubai.

Just as the two megacraft from England and France passed through the Strait of Gibraltar into the Mediterranean, Nikki flew to Athens, Greece to board the HSC purchased from Hellenic Seaways at the port city of Piraeus. The next day the megacraft (they become megayachts when outfitted by the Prince) formed a flotilla, almost a 1,000 feet in length, headed to the Suez Canal. Two days later the three craft were skimming above the waves as they rounded the Saudi Arabian peninsula into the Persian Gulf. On the fifth day, the flotilla was safely docked at Dubai's Maritime City. During the voyage, Nikki had walked all around the vessel, but she still couldn't fathom what the Prince was going to do with such a cavernous cargo deck with a capacity of 600 tons.

The next day, Prince Khalid arrived with an entourage of media personnel to welcome the HSC's and their crews during an official dedication of the new retrofit facility. A team of thirty engineers and technicians from Tasmania were in attendance.

As the Prince delivered his short remarks: "a very important day in the history of the UAE," the three captains, Prince Latif, Dahlia, Nikki and two Israelis sat behind the lectern under a canvas canopy. Prince Khalid proudly announced that the hulls would be painted dark blue and that in 18 months he would re-christen the megayachts: "Blue Clipper I, II and III." He was going to call them "Blue Genius" but was talked out of it by Prince Latif as being too revealing. The captains were interviewed by the press and gave details about the ships and their performance. No details about the use of the re-fitted craft were released. Indeed, Captain Crowley remained conspicuously quiet when asked about the Prince's project. However, he did report: "the HSC was the most seaworthy vessel he'd had the pleasure to command during his 33 years at sea." After the ceremony, an elaborate buffet was opened in a nearby air-conditioned tent. With only 11 feet of draft, the audience saw the massive HSC's winched and pushed up into their re-fit shelters.

With the final payment wired to a Swiss bank, the official celebration dinner at the Oberoi Hotel could commence. The Princes and their Blue Teams came down from the 26th floor suite to welcome the guests. The obligatory ice sculpture of an HSC gleamed in the middle of the ballroom, much to the pleasure of the guests from Tasmania. Nikki and her bosses from London sat at the head table. Dr. St. John was also a guest who quietly assured the Princes that the three purchases had been successfully crated and would arrive at the Maritime City in 30 days as promised. The merriment continued until late in the evening. Prince Khalid and Dahlia left for the mansion around 10:30. The Captains, splendid in their pure white uniforms, danced with their wives. The Tasmanians sponsored a Fosters Beer

Suite under the watchful eye of Foster York. Prince Latif was seen escorting Nikki into the elevator around 11:00.

As the couple left the elevator and entered the Prince's suite, Yousif told Nikki that she had been on his mind ever since his shadow covered her bronze body on the Dardanelle. He took her hand and walked her over to the window with a perfect view of the Burj Khalifa. He embraced her and whispered in her ear that they should get into more comfortable clothing. Nikki excused herself and found red lace underwear on the bed, just her size. A warm flush came over her whole body. After a couple of sips of cognac, the couple fell into each other's arms and kissed. The Prince put his hand on her left breast and could feel her nipple harden with excitement. Soon the couple was between the grey silk sheets mating in a most amorous fashion. Indeed, the couple made love like it was their last day on Earth. But as they feel asleep in each other's embrace, they both knew it would not be their last time together. They were too much alike to let someone or something come between them.

6

MEGAYACHT

With the three HSC's and the three Blue Gene computers purchased, the second of four phases of the prince's masterplan commenced. Phase two required the HSC's to be refitted in Dubai, complete a full data center on the cargo deck housing the supercomputer. With the three HSC's housed in the air-conditioned refit facilities, the work began modifying the massive ferryboats into classy megayachts suitable for a billionaire.

Scores of oriental workers, in part managed by the Aussies from Tasmania, swarmed aboard and around the three vessels. Storage facilities contained fine woods, paneling, marble slabs, chandeliers, furniture, galley equipment, communications systems and the thousands of items necessary to outfit a megayacht in the $200 million class vessel. Representatives from British and Italian interior design houses were busy ordering materials and directing their installations.

A Blue Clippper is a huge craft, 315 feet long and 88 feet wide. It would take eight months, working day and night, to transform the ferryboat. And the three decks rise above the water for 84 feet or the equivalent of an 8-story building. Below the water line, the engine room was painted white prior to the refurbishment of the three water jet engines with their new turbo thrusters. To complement this activity, new fuel cells were installed which would contain a novel hybrid fuel enabling additional thrust. The goal was to propel the huge vessel at sustained speeds of 48 knots.

On the cargo deck the key activity was to install a data center with an 80- foot by 45-foot glass enclosure, complete with a raised floor to accommodate the cooling pipes and power cables. The center also has a Halon fire suppression system. The cargo deck also contains two giant battery enclosures capable of generating 1.2 megawatts of electricity for a period of up to fifteen minutes. The back of the deck is a large, reinforced ramp for loading vehicles, tenders and inflatable, ribbed runabout watercraft.

A spiral staircase was installed that connected the cargo deck with the personnel deck and the bridge. Bow thrusters were installed for ease of docking.

The Blue Clippers personnel deck contains the owner's suite at the bow. It is sumptuous with a king-size bed, double bath, sauna and exercise room. Dark woods are complemented by white furniture and pale blue curtains. Two of the three suites were furnished with Prince Khalid's favorite colors and one was furnished with Prince Latif's favorite colors. Both schemes were predominantly blue and gold. This deck also contains a central hallway leading to the crew and visitor staterooms. Dahlia has her own stateroom decorated in purple and white fabrics. The three Israelis also had the pleasure of decorating their private spaces. The seventeen crew members were treated to a large salon and dining room opposite a modern, stainless steel galley. At the stern of the personnel's middle deck is a small gym, swimming pool and movie theater.

The upper deck contains the bridge with a 180-degree panoramic view and a leather bench for visitors to watch helm operations. Behind the bridge is the Captain's Quarters with a small chart room and the Communications and Information Center (CIC) with its direct links to the communications systems and radars mounted on masts above. This deck also contains staterooms for the First Mate and the Chief Engineer. Two hotel suites are also available for VIP's. A 20-foot by 12-foot swimming pool is in the center of the deck with a Jacuzzi and swim-up bar. The entire deck is ringed with teak flooring and walkways. From the stern railing, operations on the helideck can be observed.

The hull is painted dark blue with the upper decks a bright yellow that gleams in the Middle Eastern sun and glows at sunrise and sunset. Aqua lights mounted all around the craft just below the waterline provide an aura of light blue clouds surrounding the clipper.

With the painting complete and most of the carpentry complete, the computer room was sanitized for the installation of the Blue Gene. The assembly of the huge supercomputer with its 64 racks of equipment could begin. A cluster of technicians from IBM were required for this 2-month task. Each equipment rack was wheeled into the center, mounted in place and the electrical connections completed. The racks were connected to a main console with huge cables running under the floor. IBM engineers could be seen in the glass-enclosed conference room detailing the test regimes necessary for the machine's sell-off prior to the sea trails.

Exactly eighteen months to the day, Prince Khalid led a party of distinguished guests to the royal blue canopy on the pier to participate in the christening of the new megayachts. With all three vessels lined up at the Maritime City's pier, several speeches were given about the Blue Clippers and the impact on the megayacht production potential of the Maritime City. Key guests were given tours of the personnel and bridge decks. The cargo decks were off-limits. The Australians from INCAT, including their boss, Foster York, were congratulated for their roles. IBM executives were quietly in the background still wondering why their beautiful machines were going to sea.

As Dahlia broke a champagne bottle on the bow of Blue Clipper I, Prince Latif thanked the crowd for witnessing such an important event in the history of the UAE and said: "With Allah's help, may the sea trials be successful."

7

SEA TRIALS

As the three Blue Clippers let the Maritime City for different test ranges agreed upon by the survey team, the megayachts churned the water of the Persian Gulf, although nobody aboard called it that. On board were independent, experienced survey teams commissioned by Lloyds of London to certify every aspect of the seaworthiness of the Prince's flotilla.

Twenty miles out to sea, the survey team captain informed the Skippers that all teams and systems were a "Go" for commencing the trails. Each captain then asked his crew: "Are you ready to commence the sea trails?" The crews of Blue Clipper I, II and III responded with an "Aye, Aye, Skipper!" Captain Crowley's Clipper had a secure satellite link to Prince Latif's suite in the Oberoi Hotel. The Prince knew what was happening at all times. Indeed, nothing was left to chance. The Prince could view the survey teams and related instruments via a closed-circuit television link. The Prince had also commissioned occasional helicopter over-flights to monitor the speed trails in the event of a controversy.

For each Blue Clipper three days of prescribed activities would thoroughly test all of the systems and subsystems on board except one, the supercomputer. It had its own set of test engineers to check the operation, even in high waves. The purpose was to give the Prince high confidence that the supercomputer would complete its mission at a pier or, if necessary, in a harbor. Dahlia was aboard Blue Clipper I to test lavatory and galley functions. Two hours into the first day of testing, she reported to the Prince: "Your Highness, all systems are a "Go." "Indeed, this yacht feels like a home away from home. The Aussies, the Brits and the Italians all did their jobs exceptionally well.

I think you'll be pleased, Your Highness." The Prince smiled as he surveyed other monitors in his suite.

The survey teams consisted of a Lead (usually a senior sea captain known to Lloyds of London) and an expert in each of the following areas: superstructure/hull, Navigation and Electronics, Engine Room, Nautical maneuvers and safety systems. The cargo deck was off-limits except for access to the engine room. In all of the clippers, the test team noticed the stabilization effect of a huge payload in the center of the lower deck. For three days and night, sensor systems were hooked up to the:

-Hull and superstructure including anchor systems, steering elements, bow and stern thrusters, water jets, davits and bilge pumping systems. Non-destructive tests were performed on the exhaust systems and navigation lights.

-Navigation & Communications systems. Interference was interjected into the communications systems to verify voice and data throughput. The radars were tested for accuracy via GPS downlinks. The autopilot system was tested in accordance with the calibration data provided by the manufacturer. Tests were run on the chart plotters and all of the display screens.

-Nautical Trails consisted of a series of speed trails in different maneuvers at different speeds including dead ship recovery. Stopping, starting and backing maneuvers were verified.

-Engine Room verification included engine operation, temperature, noise, lubricant leak, vibration, hydraulic pressure, propeller speeds, impact of gearing and cooling.

At 4:00 PM on the third day of the trials, the survey team informed the Captains that the trails were completed and that the megacraft could return to the Maritime city. By midnight each craft was in position at the pier as the teams unloaded their sensor equipment. In the background, the Blue Gene test team also unloaded their gear and quietly made their way to their hotel. Captain Crowley monitored the system closures from the bridge. As he walked out to the docking platform, he noticed his survey team Captain saluting the bow of Blue Clipper I. In the nautical world, this usually meant: "I salute you, and you are ready to ply the blue domain." The Captain sleep very well that night.

Three weeks after the trails, the official report was e-mailed to Prince Latif. It included the data and photographic archive about the systems and subsystems, the data from oil, water and fluid samples, fuel consumption, navigation accuracy readings and electrical systems with all exceeding the specifications. The report highlighted the Clipper's seaborne maneuvers with "a speed and stability, uncommon in the realm of megayachts." Upon reading the report, Prince Latif only made one phone call: "Hello, Dr. St. John, how did our machines do during the sea trials?

"Your Highness, I am very pleased to report that each Blue Gene exceeded the warranty parameters, and you have three operational supercomputers for whatever your use."

The Prince responded: "Thank you, Sir. Please send the data directly to me, and I will promptly remit the remaining payment."

"I will do so, Your Highness," replied the IBM salesman. "And may this compute power serve some worthy purpose."

On the other end of the line, the Prince thought to himself: "Oh, it will. Believe me; it will."

With the Clippers now deemed seaworthy and insured by Lloyds of London, the Prince was almost ready to commence Phase 3 of his project.

8

CELEBRATION

Prince Latif was almost ready to commence Phase 3. But before he could celebrate, he wanted assurances from Captain Crowley and Dr. Raviv that both the ship and the computer were up to the task for a successful mission.

At 8:00 AM on the day after the HSC's arrived at the Maritime city, the Prince called "Catfish": "Skipper, I need to talk with you and Adam at 8:30 this morning on your bridge. Please alert Adam and meet me there."

"Will, do, Sir," replied the Skipper. "We'll be there."

Promptly at 8:20, the Prince's Maybach pulled up to Blue Clipper I which looked majestic in the morning sun. Within 10 minutes the Prince reached the bridge where the seaman and computer guru were waiting.

"Guys," began the Prince. "We're about to celebrate the sea trail success and commence Phase 3 of our mission. I must be absolutely sure we're ready. I hope you understand." The captain looked at Catfish who said: "Well, Sir, I personally went over the numbers in the survey Report. This vessel meets or exceeds all the established criteria. I have full confidence in the performance of our Clippers."

"Fine, Sir, I respect your experience in this regard," replied the Prince as he turned to the Israeli. "Adam, do you have the same level of confidence about the Blue Gene as the skipper has for the megayachts?"

Dr. Raviv didn't hesitate for a moment: "Yes, Sir, I do." "The computer used less power than anticipated, but the throughput was the same as a land-based machine. I have full confidence the Blue Genes will be ready to perform their missions."

"And what about the machine's ability to process encryption algorithms?" asked the Prince.

"Your Highness, we've run simulations on encryption codes which are much more difficult than the ones we'll face on the missions. I am confident we'll break the codes in the time allotted or less," stated Dr. Raviv with an air of uncommon confidence which pleased the Prince.

"Very well then," replied the Prince. "We'll party tonight and depart at 7:00 AM on Friday." The Prince shook the hand of his key employees and quickly descended the spiral staircase.

The Oberoi Hotel was ready to meet every demand for a grand celebration prior to the departure of the Clippers. Key INCAT and IBM engineers and technicians found themselves in royal suites overlooking the Dubai city center and mall. Hourly busses took crews to and from the gold souk. VIP tours were arranged to visit the Observation Deck of the El Burj Khalifa on the 124th floor of the world's tallest building. In the evening, a grand circular buffet ringed the obligatory ice sculpture of a Clipper. The speeches were brief as Prince Khalid thanked the teams for making the schedule and creating incredible megayachts.

"I promise an even bigger celebration upon the completion of our missions," said Prince Latif. The 100-person gathering enthusiastically clapped its appreciation. Large cooling fans were set up on the terrace so revelers could enjoy cigars and cognac with soft music provided by a trio in the background.

Prince Latif shook the hand of Foster York of INCAT and Dr. St. John of IBM as he departed the fete with his friend from Monaco.

On Friday, right on schedule, Prince Khalid and his entourage were present at the pier as Captain Crowley's Blue Clipper I blew its horn three time to indicate the flotilla's departure. At the same time,

Prince Latif's Gulfstream took off for Monaco to ensure that the operations for a successful mission were underway.

Twenty miles out to sea, the three captains opened their instruction envelopes to find out that:

- Blue Clipper I was bound for Bermuda
- Blue Clipper II was bound for Cabo San Lucas
- Blue Clipper III was bound for Monaco

Eight days later, the Blue clippers were in their assigned ports, refueled and ready for their missions.

9

AMBULANCES

As the Prince's business jet touched down at the Aeroport Nice Conte d'Azur, the Prince telephoned his contact in Nice: "Jacques, are you ready to show me the vehicle," he asked.

"Yes, sir," was the response. "We're located at 26 Rue Marceau just one block east of the main railroad station," came a woman's voice over the secure telephone link.

Ten minutes later a black van pulled up to the warehouse, and the driver was instructed to stay for one-half hour. The garage door opened, and a dashing Frenchman stretched out his hand to greet the Prince.

"Bon jour, Your Highness," said Jacques Malreau as he quickly motioned for the Prince to step inside as he pulled down the garage door.

About twenty feet inside was a gleaming red and white Mercedes Benz ambulance with a variety of lights and antennas on top. The former Formula 1 race car driver opened the back doors and motioned for the Prince to step inside. He did so and sat on a bench across from several communications consoles with multiple displays and keyboards.

"Sir, we've made this exactly to your specifications,' stated the Frenchman. "It has three modes of communications: microwave, GMS cellular and SATCOM, all highspeed, wide-bandwidth and secure. And we have set up a transmitter just outside the train station.

"Sir, please look at the signal strength on this monitor," continued the Frenchman. "It is the same in all three communications modes. And we're using a frequency that is rarely used by the gendarme so we will not alert anybody to our transmission. And, if we do, by the time our mission is over, we'll be long gone, and this vehicle will no longer exist."

"Excellent," responded the Prince. Now please demonstrate the link over our Desertstar satellite," asked the Prince.

"Of course, Sir," responded the responsive employee. "We've put an antenna in the window, and this line connects to the display." At that time, Monsieur Malreau typed a message on a keyboard which only a receiver on the other end of the Desertstar link would understand. A text message came back and was displayed on a monitor: "Confirm receipt of all data. Good Day."

The Prince studied the message and said:" This is a very good day. Have you done dry-runs of the route from here to the Casino Monte-Carlo?"

"Yes, Your Highness," "Here is the videotape of our last run," replied Malreau as his female partner looked on. "As you can see, the M6007 highway runs directly into the D6007 in Monaco for the seven-mile trip," responded the Frenchman as the vehicle-mounted camera showed the route. "And with sirens blaring, if necessary, we should experience minimal traffic on a holiday Monday morning, Your Highness."

At this point, the Prince got up and stepped down out of the vehicle. He then shook Jacque's hand and nodded to his partner as he said: "Good job, my friend. Please await my signal. It will come via our secure link embedded in our garbled text. Do you understand?"

"Yes, Sir," replied the Frenchman. "You pay us handsomely, and we will be ready when you call."

"Thank you and Good Bye," was the Prince's short reply as he turned and left the building. An hour later, the Prince's Gulfstream was over the Strait of Gibraltar headed for New York City.

Five hours later the Prince's jet landed at the Newark International Airport in New Jersey and taxied to the commercial aviation hangar. A limousine than whisked him to a warehouse in Fort Hamilton south of Brooklyn, New York. As the limousine pulled up to the building, Steven Goldman, a long-time friend of the Prince's from college days, walked out and shook His Highness's hand as he escorted him into the garage. The conversation started about the good old days but quickly turned to business as the Prince approached a red and white ambulance. Mr. Goldman then beckoned the Prince to climb inside for the demonstration of communications links and throughput rates. After witnessing the same structured demonstration as in Nice, the Prince remarked: "Steven, you've done it. It performs per specification in both directions to and from Dubai. Your efforts are truly appreciated, my friend," continued the Prince. "How is the drive from here to lower Manhatten?"

"It's easy, Sir," replied Mr. Goldman. "We simply go north on Route 278 to 478 through the Hugh Carey tunnel to FDR Drive east to Broad Street which goes directly to our target. It's also convenient because we can turn on Maiden Lane and go directly to Pier 15 River Esplanade." "Would you like to see the video, Sir?" asked the New Yorker.

"No, that won't be necessary, Steven," replied the Prince. "I trust you and your wife, Audrey. Please give her my regards." "Please wait for my signal to proceed." With that the Prince of Dubai left the building and motored back to the airport. An hour later, his jet was at 30,000 feet headed to San Francisco.

The Prince's whirlwind journey took another five hours to get to San Francisco's International Airport due to strong headwinds. The Prince called ahead to confirm the readiness for his visit. He wasn't disappointed.

Fifteen minutes after landing, the Prince's limousine pulled up to a single story warehouse on Cargo Way, just east of 3rd Street in the Hunter's Point section of South San Francisco. As the limo pulled up, out came another trusted friend of Prince Latif, Nathan Kalish, a 39-year old Porsche salesman from Redondo Beach, California.

The two men recalled a couple happy moments while attending UCLA as they walked up to an ambulance. Kalish's demonstration was just like the previous two. It proved the two-way, redundant, secure communications link between the ambulance and Pier 3 of the Embarcadero as well as via satellite relay to Dubai. Mr. Kalish also convinced the Prince that the 3rd street location was perfect for access into the Financial District. The Prince asked his friend to wait for his coded text signal and parted with an invitation to Dubai "when our little adventure is over." Mr. Kalish eagerly accepted the offer.

Only two hours later, the Prince's Gulfstream was airborne, this time headed south to Cabo San Lucas in Mexico to inspect a marina and take a few days to meet Ms. Katie Flynn, the 32-year old Marina Manager/Harbormaster who made a global reputation by sailing solo from Cabo to Indonesia. As the plane turned south, just over the Golden Gate Bridge, the Prince put his head back on a pillow, and a sly smile came over his face.

10

CABO SAN LUCAS

As the Prince's jet circled over the end of Mexico's Baja California Peninsula, the famous landmark of the sea arch called El Arco de Cabo San Lucas could be seen. The harbor was bustling with pleasure boats, wind surfers, fishing boats and cruise ships. The plane landed at the Los Cabos International Airport where the Prince found his transportation for the 6-mile trip to the Hotel Riu Palace Cabo San Lucas, a stunning structure on the ocean drive of Camino Viejo a San Jose.

It was early afternoon when the Prince called Ms. Flynn to arrange a visit that afternoon at 4:00 PM. The Harbormaster had been alerted of the Prince's visit via email from Dubai. Promptly at 4:00, the Prince, splendid in a pure while linen Kaftan, knocked on the Harbormaster's door. Katie Flynn, a trim, 32-year old fitness instructor with a bronzed body and wide smile, welcomed His Highness to Cabo.

"Your Highness, I've eagerly awaited your arrival," said Katie. "Your assistant, Ms. Samira, emailed that you need a pier for your vessel."

"That's right, Ms. Flynn," replied the Prince. "Indeed, the craft, the Blue Clipper II, is on its way to this marina as we speak."

"What is the size or class of your vessel, Your Highness," inquired Ms. Flynn.

"Well, it's very large, 315 feet by 88 feet. From what I can see, I would need the external position on your N Pier,' replied the Prince.

"Oh, I see." "and how long would your need it?" asked the Harbormaster.

"Starting next Sunday, I would need it for a month. We would be here for a week, then depart for three days and return for another three weeks," responded the Prince. "Is the N Pier available?" he asked.

Ms. Flynn accessed her tablet and moments later confirmed its availability.

"Would you like to inspect it now?" she asked the Prince. Yes, I would if it's not an inconvenience for you," replied the Prince.

Katie locked the office door, and the two hopped in a golf cart and headed down the pier.

"Your Highness, Sir, at 315 feet your yacht is a small ocean liner. It must be quite a sight and pleasure to be aboard," stated Ms. Flynn with an inquiring mind.

"Well, it's brand new, and I've hardly stepped foot aboard, much less taken a cruise," replied the Prince.

Katie parked the golf cart in the middle of the N pier and explained the hook-ups--water, power, cable television and pump-out services available. "And, Your Highness, our fee is by length with very few extra charges or taxes," assured the Harbormaster.

"That's agreeable to me under one condition," replied the Prince.

"What's that, Sir?" May I ask?" inquired the youthful, albeit seasoned mariner.

"That you be my quest for dinner this evening and moral support at the Players Casino afterwards," said the Prince expecting a positive response to his invitation.

"Well tonight is my night off, and I'd be honored, Your Highness," replied Ms. Flynn.

"Oh, and I have another favor," replied the Prince.

"What's that, Your Highness?" asked Katie.

"That in private your please address me as Yousif," replied the Prince.

"Well, Sir...I mean Yousif..I'll try to remember to do so," responded Katie with a broad grin.

"Please do try," replied the Prince.

As they took the golf cart back to the office, the Prince said: "Ms. Flynn please have the papers ready for me to sign this evening. My car will pick you up here at 7:30, if that's agreeable with you?" asked the Prince.

"Yes, Sir, Your Highness…I mean Yousif," "I'll be ready with the papers at 7:30," replied Katie with real excitement in her voice. As they parted ways, Katie was sure that the one-month slip fee would go a long way toward balancing her budget.

Prince Latif was waiting in the Hotel lobby when Katie arrived. She looked like a bronze Goddess in her spaghetti strap red sequin dress showing only a modest amount of cleavage. She walked with confidence in her red high heels as she reached out to shake the Prince's hand and politely bowed her head.

The Prince was quick to respond: "I've been around the world, but you're the prettiest Harbormaster I've ever seen."

Katie blushed at the complement.

Only moments later the couple was sitting by the window in the main dining room bathed by glow of the setting sun. Prince Latif took a quick look at the Contract document and asked: "Are there any ugly penalty clauses of which I should be aware?"

"No, Yousif, it's very straight-forward if the payments are made on time but with a standard grace period," replied the Harbormaster.

"Very well," said the Prince as he pulled out his Montblanc pen and signed the document. He then attached a business card and asked that a copy be faxed to the Dubai address on the card.

Over a lobster dinner, the Prince found out a lot about the young lady as she recalled her ocean voyages and corporate experiences. He found many of the same qualities in Katie that he had experienced in Nikki Villefranche. After a light lime flan dessert, the Prince asked Katie if she were still willing to accompany him to the small casino on Paseo de la Marina.

"Sure, it sounds fun, but I warn you, my limit is only to bet twenty dollars an evening," replied Katie.

"Ha-Ha, "replied the Prince. "That's quite ok. I think you'll bring me good luck."

The Prince was right. As Katie stood by his side at the Blackjack table, his chips were piled up in neat stacks. Once, when the Prince hit a big jackpot, Katie put her arm around the   Prince's waist as they jumped for joy. She quickly pulled back her arm and apologized for the outburst.

"Opps, Sorry, Sir," she said. The Prince patted her on the shoulder and smiled. After only one hour, the casino manager was relieved to see the couple go out the front door to an awaiting black limousine. Only a few minutes later, the car pulled up to the Marina's gate.

"Katie," said the Prince. "I've decided to stay until Sunday in order to see the Blue Clipper arrive. And I'd love to give you a tour of her."

'Yousif, that's really good news. I'd love to get a tour. And since you're here another day, I'd love to take you out on my tender to show you the Arco, our famous tourist attraction," said Katie.

"That's an offer I can't refuse,' Said the Prince. "Are you sure you can take the time off to do so?" asked the Prince.

"Sure, I've got a lot of overtime leave due me, and I need a break," replied Katie.

"Just let me know when, and I'll bring a picnic lunch," replied Yousif as he leaned over and gently patted Katie on the side of her head.

At noon on Friday, Katie's 16-foot go-fast tender pulled up to the dock at the Hotel Riu Palace. She helped Yousif board the boat and place the picnic cooler under a seat. She adroitly backed-up the boat, turned around and pushed the throttle forward. In no time the boat was speeding along at 35 knots. They would occasionally hit a wake of another go-fast boat when the Prince enjoyed Katie's bounding breasts hardly covered by a bright orange bikini top. After circling around the famous Arco arch, the Prince took a couple photos with his cell phone and took care to include Katie in the field of view.

As they rounded the southern-most point of the Baja peninsula, Katie slowed the craft and anchored a few feet from a sandy beach.

"You'll never guess the name of this beach," as she tempted Yousif for an answer.

"I give up," replied the Arab gentleman.

"Divorce Beach," replied Katie as she giggled.

"Oh," replied Yousif. "And I suppose there's a Marriage Beach somewhere around here."

"No, smartie," replied Katie, "but around the cove is "Lover's Beach.""

They both laughed as Yousif took off his trousers revealing a very athletic set of legs earned by many polo matches. The couple jumped in the water with the plastic cooler floating between them as they waded ashore.

Only a few other couples were on the beach, all separated for privacy. Yousif and Katie found a quiet grotto, laid out a blanket and enjoyed a champagne lunch. Several times the couple walked along the shallow surf when at one point the Prince held out his hand to hold Katie's hand. Hand-in-hand they searched for small shells and minnows. At times, they ribbed suntan oil on each other. After three hours, they "wondered where the time went" and pulled the anchor to head back to the hotel. As the Prince stepped onto the pier, he said: "Katie you're really special. I had a great time! I would be honored to treat you to dinner, perhaps a tiki bar of your choosing."

"Well, Yousif, you beat me to the punch as we Americans say," responded Katie. "I was going to ask you to be my guest at the Cabo Wabo Cantina."

"Sounds fun. That's right downtown near the casino, isn't it?" asked the Prince, who had obviously done his homework.

"Yes. I'll reserve a table for 7:00 PM, and please Yousif be casual," replied Katie. Both looked forward to the dinner date. Yousif stood on the pier to watch Katie speed away.

On Sunday in the warm afternoon sun, you would have thought the people tending their vessels in the marina were witnessing a tsunami wave as the enormous Blue Clipper II entered the harbor. It was like a cruise ship, but alas it was a private megayacht with its shiny dark blue hull and yellow topside. As it slowly bow-thrusted toward the pier, the golf cart carrying Katie and the Prince arrived. Prince Latif waved to Captain Caselli who was leaning over the bridge docking platform.

"Wow," exclaimed Katie. "I knew it would be huge the way you described it, Prince, but I had no idea it would be THIS large!" "What is the size of the crew?"

"Only seventeen," replied the Prince with real pride. "We've automated many functions." The pair waited for the gangplank to be lowered and then were greeted by the Captain as they stepped aboard.

"How was your trip?" asked the Prince.

"Your Highness, it performed flawlessly and is a true pleasure to pilot," responded Captain Caselli.

"Excellent," replied the Prince as he introduced Katie as the Harbormaster.

"Welcome aboard, Miss." "We'll try to be good tenants for about a month," said the Captain.

"I'm going to give her a tour topside," said the Prince. "And maybe even convince her to stay for dinner," said the Prince.

Katie followed the Prince to the spiral staircase and was motioned by him to take the lead climbing the steps inlaid with crystal chips. Halfway up to the bridge, she stopped and turned around to say: "Your Highness, I think I'm getting altitude sickness!" They both laughed as they made it to the bridge with its long row of instruments and 180- degree wrap-around panoramic view. Captain Caselli then explained the purpose of many of the instruments and was delighted by the keen questioning by the Harbormaster. He complemented her on her knowledge as the Prince beckoned her to continue the tour.

"Skipper, please plan to join us for dinner at 7:30," said the Prince, as the couple descended the staircase.

"Of course, Sir." "We'll have something special for our guest," answered the Captain.

On the middle deck the couple walked down the teakwood central hallway past a series of staterooms into the grand salon. With a baby grand piano in the corner and several leather sofas forming conversation areas, the guest could hardly believe her eyes. She had seen rooms like this in Show Boat magazines, but this was for real. She inspected the galley with all of its stainless steel appliances. She was impressed by the 12-foot dining table with its center formed by a backlit slab of onyx. The combination of the dark woods and the light fabrics bathed in light by the large windows also impressed the Harbormaster. Then the Prince led his guest into his Dubai bedroom suite, complete with double bathrooms and office. On the king size bed lay an orange bikini. He motioned for Katie to come over and examine it. "It's mine!" she exclaimed.

"No, it isn't but the same size, model and color," replied the Prince in a reassuring tone.

"I thought we could go for a swim prior to dinner," the Prince continued. The pool and hot tub are on the upper bridge deck, complete with a swim-up minibar."

"Well, you certainly have a flair for entertaining, Yousif," responded Katie with a twinkle in her eye.

They both put on their bathing suits and climbed the staircase up to the top of the megacraft. After a couple minutes of splashing each other like kids, they climbed out of the pool and stepped down into the hot tub. As the water jets melted away pain, Katie thought to herself: "I could really fit into this lifestyle." As they dried themselves, a steward approached them for a drink order. Katie ordered a Pina Colada and the Prince said: "Make that two, please." For an hour they swam, chatted, enjoyed cocktails and watched the sun slip below the horizon.

"Let's get dressed for dinner, Katie" said Yousif.

"Wait a minute, Yousif, I only have the clothes I wore on the pier," responded Katie. Then she paused a slight moment and continued: "Don't tell me you have my size of dress and shoes in the bedroom."

The Prince smiled and quietly said: "Let's go find out."

The pair then went downstairs to the Dubai suite.

"I think you'll find something you'll like hanging in the bathroom and the shoes are on the bench," stated Prince Latif with some certainty.

Katie went into the bathroom and exclaimed, "Oh, my God!" as she returned to the bedroom holding up a strapless, silver Chanel Haute Couture evening gown. She put it over her bodice and held it at the waist as she spun around in a gleeful circle.

"Yousif, it's gorgeous." "This dinner is going to be a real treat I can tell already," as she smiled and walked over to the Prince and gave him a peck on the cheek.

"I'm glad you like it, my dear," replied Yousif. "You'll find other treats in the bathroom, including your toiletries." The Captain and First Mate will join us for cocktails at 7:30."

"I'll be ready!!" responded the flirtatious Harbormaster.

There were many people on the Blue Clipper II, but Katie never saw them; it was the crew doing their duties.

She left the Dubai suite and joined her hosts in the grand salon. As she entered the room, the Prince, dressed in a white silk Kaftan, glided over to her, and held out his elbow to escort her to the other end of the salon to meet the Captain and the First Mate, both looking regal in their summer white uniforms. She felt like the belle of the ball as the party of four sipped champagne and ate delicate canopies. Promptly at 8:00PM they sat down at one end of the dining table with the Prince on the end and the seamen across from Katie. Over a sumptuous Rack of Lamb dinner, the conversation was all about the sea complete with real-life stories. The Captain and First mate were enthralled by Katie's description of her solo Pacific Ocean crossing. The Prince didn't have much to say; he didn't need to. After dinner the party moved to a U-shaped conversation area for small after dinner cordials. At 10:00 the Captain and First Mate excused themselves: "as duty calls."

"I know tomorrow is a workday for you, Katie," said Yousif. "But I really don't want you to go." "In a perfect world"..just then Katie put her index finger to the Prince's lips..and finished the sentence: "you would spend the night here."

The prince looked her in the eye and said: "Yes."

"Well, if that's an invitation, then I accept," said Katie in a rather sultry tone.

The couple then got up and walked arm-in-arm down the hall to the Dubai suite where the bed was already turned down and small candles placed on several window sills.

In the middle of the room, Katie turned to Yousif and lowered her dress to the floor. They embraced as their lips met in a soulful kiss and her bra was adroitly unhooked. The couple went over to the bed, sat down and continued undressing. They exchanged soft words of admiration as the Prince-now really feeling like Yousif the MAN-tenderly touched her breasts and heightened nipples. They slid between the silk sheets and locked in a tight embrace of mutual delight. The new partners explored mutually-pleasing positions into the early morning. They both realized that the moment was very special and never to be forgotten.

The next morning as he climbed into his Gulfstream, the prince texted Katie that he would return to her arms before many moons had passed.

11

BERMUDA

On a rainy, chilly morning, Blue Clipper I under the command of Catfish Crowley departed Cork, Ireland for the Royal Navy Dockyard in Bermuda. The voyage was within the range of the megayacht provided the weather was favorable and high sea state waves didn't require burning more fuel. Indeed, on this voyage, the Gulf Stream current allowed a couple more knots to the vessel's speed. During the four-day trip, the Blue Gene team ran numerous routines to confirm its ability to detect and neutralize computer encryption algorithms. Blue Clipper II had already run the routines while passing through the Panama Canal on the way to Cabo and provided the findings to Blue Clipper I via secure satellite link.

While the megayacht was a day away from Bermuda, the Prince's jet touched down at the airport serving Hamilton, Bermuda's capital city. A shuttle from the Rosedon Hotel on Rosemont Avenue picked up His Highness. On the front porch of the hotel was Win Parker, the Maritime Harbormaster waiting for the Prince. Captain Parker, a 20-year veteran nautical engineer with the Royal Navy and a member of Britain's team racing for America's Cup, reminds one of the actor George Clooney.

The Prince's limousine pulled up to the hotel and was met by the doorman. As Prince Latif came up the stairs, Harbormaster Parker went down to greet the Prince.

"Welcome to Bermuda, Your Highness. We eagerly await your vessel," said Mr. Parker with an outstretched hand.

"I'm glad to be here, Mr. Parker, and learn about your dockyard complex," replied the Prince.

Soon they were in the lobby being served tea as they discussed the Prince's requirements. "Except for the cruise ships, our Blue Clipper

I will look like a battleship coming into your facility. It's not only long but 88 feet wide. My research shows that you only have one pier that can accommodate it. I hope we can be a tenant for a month," continued the Prince.

"Yes, Your Highness, we have reserved it for your vessel and will run frequent buses from the pier to here in Hamilton to accommodate your crew," replied the Harbormaster. "And I've arranged a reception party because your Skipper Crowley and I are long-time friends. I knew Tom when he piloted Caribbean cruise ships through here."

"Excellent, Mr. Parker. "I believe we made the right choice to have Bermuda as our home port," replied the Prince. "Can you give me a tour this afternoon?"

"Of course, Sir, when will it be convenient for you?" asked the Harbormaster.

"Let's say 3:00 PM for an hour or so," responded the Prince.

"It will be done, Your Highness," said the Harbormaster as he stood up, shook the Prince's hand, nodded his head in respect and left the hotel.

For the next day and one-half, the Prince toured the Dockyard, the Hamilton waterfront and some of the tourist sites on the twenty square-mile island. At night, he took his meal on the veranda as he kept in contact with his three Clippers.

As the sun rose on his third day on the island, the Prince stood on the Pier to welcome the Blue Clipper I. Right on schedule, Captain Crowley's big, blue baby enter the harbor. It was a thrilling sight as the Harbormaster had arranged for 2 fireboats to shoot their water cannons on each side of the megayacht. The Prince smiled with delight, and the Skipper could be seen waving from the docking platform. One person in the longshoreman group assembled on the pier was overheard asking, "How can one man own something so large and beautiful?"

As promised, that evening the Harbormaster held a reception for the crew at the National Museum of Bermuda, only five blocks from the Blue Clipper I. Afterwards, the Prince joined Captain Crowley in his chart room to get briefed on his ocean crossing.

"Your Highness," began the Skipper, "this craft has exceeded all of our requirements. It is so fast, yet so stable and more efficient than we initially planned. Being on a ship of this caliber should have little impact upon our Blue Gene cargo."

"That's just what I wanted to hear, Tom" replied Prince Latif. "Please ready the ship for the mission next week."

Just then came a knock on the cabin door. "Come in," said the Captain.

Adam Raviv opened the door and entered room by excusing his intrusion. He saluted the Prince, and said he would be brief. "I just wanted to express my appreciation to the Skipper, and now to you, Your Highness, for the marvelous environment created for the supercomputer. All of our systems are a "go" Sir, and I have the data logs to prove it," reported the computer guru.

"So there's no change in our Concept of Operations (CONOPS)?" asked the Prince.

"No, Sir, we are ready to start the mission," stated Raviv with certainty.

"Perfect," replied the Prince. "The two of you will join me for dinner at the Rosedon Hotel tonight at 6:00 PM. And please give the crew the day off tomorrow to enjoy Hamilton but warn them that everything is very expensive."

"Will do," the Captain and the guru replied in unison.

After shopping in Hamilton's tourist shops on Pitts Bay Road, Raviv's two cyber-specialists, Amy and Amira, enjoyed a traditional tea service at a sidewalk café. Amy Grossberg, a blackbelt in Kung Fu, and Amira Atara, a banking industry security expert who remined one of the actress, Natalie Portman, sat next to each other, their thighs often touching under the table. As the wind blew Amy's long black hair across her face, Amira gently swept it back with the back of her hand. Both seem oblivious of the passers-by as they held each other's hand on the table top.

At 6:00 PM, the Captain in his crisp summer white uniform and Dov Raviv wearing white trousers and a blue silk shirt with yellow hibiscus blossoms, walked up to the Prince's poolside table in the Rosedon's courtyard. The Prince motioned for his guests to have a seat. Drink orders were taken as the Prince opened the conversation by saying: "we're alone out here, and I'm reasonably sure nobody can hear our conversation. So both of you be candid and forthright with any comments or criticism, our mission may depend upon it. Is that clear?"

The Captain and Raviv looked at each other and responded affirmatively: "Yes,Sir!"

"Very well, then," replied the Prince. "I want to be absolutely sure we have the right CONOPS as we will implant the cellphones one week from today in New York and San Francisco and ten days from now in Monaco."

Then the Prince addressed Dr. Raviv, "You and your team invented and demonstrated the ability of a cellphone to exploit electromagnetic radiation (EMR) to force a computer's memory bus to function like an antenna to wirelessly broadcast data to a cellphone over cellular frequencies. You call it GSMem: Data Exfiltration from Air-Gapped Computers. Am I correct so far?" asked the Prince.

"Yes, sir," replied Raviv. "And our software is embedded in the baseband firmware of a cellphone which is placed near a data center. In short, we don't need to be in the computer room to extract data. All we need is to bypass the encryption and activate the cellphone in an extraction mode."

"And," continued the Prince, "the Blue Gene L computer can discover and bypass the encryption in a matter of a few minutes, right?"

"Yes, Sir," replied the obedient Israeli. "And we haven't seen an encryption code yet that we can't break. In fact, we ran thousands of scenarios while we came here and were successful every time," stated Raviv.

"Thank you, replied the Prince. "That's what I wanted to hear. Now let's enjoy dinner."

Back on the Blue Clipper I, Amy and Amira finished dinner and were showing each other their clothing purchases in Amy's stateroom. Amira took off her blouse to try on one of her new purchases. Amy then approached her friend, put her arms around her and unhooked her bra. As the garment fell to the floor, the couple hugged and kissed each other. Within minutes the two nude women were on the bed locked in a lover's embrace with a high state of arousal. Each partner wondered why they had been friends for so long without enjoying such erotica. They fell asleep in each other's arms.

12

MONACO

A day later, the Prince's jet landed in Nice, and he was driven to the Monaco Marina Hercule to visit the Blue Clipper III for three important meetings. The first meeting took place in the Grand Salon with Captain Jolie.

"Sir," began the Skipper, "we have reviewed the data from our trip from Dubai, and I can report to you with confidence that this ship performed flawlessly. Indeed, most of the critical parameters-speed, fuel consumption, vibration and reduced electrical energy-were exceeded. Even with the Blue Gene running, there was no impact on other systems. I'm truly impressed with your vessel, Your Highness."

"Skipper, that's what I needed to hear," replied Prince Latif. "How was the passage through the Suez Canal?"

"Uneventful and very smooth, Sir," responded the seasoned captain. "We had 23 feet clearance on both sides of the Clipper."

"Excellent, Skipper," replied the Prince. Please give me a report of your consumables at the end of the week."

"Will do, Sir," as the Skipper was excused to get back to the bridge when the Prince said: "Skipper, you run a tight ship. Please continue to do so."

"Aye, aye, Sir," was the response.

What the Prince did not tell the Captain was that the only other voyage the Skipper would take on Blue Clipper III was the return to Dubai.

An hour later, the Prince asked Tom van der Heyden to join him in his office in the Dubai suite.

"Mr. van der Heyden," the Prince stated, "you're our clandestine communications expert. Are you satisfied with our cellphone device now that one has been modified per your specifications?"

"Yes, Your Highness, I am," replied the engineer. "We ran the tests during our voyage here, and the signals are even stronger than I predicted."

He continued: "With your permission, I would like to configure eight of them. Two for each city and two for our lab to trouble-shoot in the event we have a problem."

"You have my permission," responded the Prince. "And please let me know when they all pass the final tests, ideally before next Friday," instructed Prince Latif.

"Will do, Sir," was the proper response.

The third meeting that day was also very important. The Prince changed into his swimming suit, climbed up the spiral staircase and joined his friend, the yacht broker, at the minibar beside the swimming pool.

"So glad you accepted my invitation, Nikki," said the Prince with genuine sincerity.

Nikki got up from her bar stool and said in a quiet voice, "Yousif, you know when you call, I come running, my dear."

The Prince blushed for a moment and then regained his composure to ask the former model to spin around to show off her latest bikini.

"I don't know how you stay so fit, my dear, when you're always dining out with clients," said the Prince as a rhetorical question.

"Well, Yousif, you know I have small gym on my boat, and I use it!' responded Nikki.

The couple enjoyed the pool and hot tub for an hour before the Prince invited his friend to dinner.

"Your yacht or mine?" she asked.

"Neither," replied the Prince. "Let's go to the hotel and afterwards spend an hour at the casino.

56

"And I suppose I have an outfit ready in your suite? She asked.

"You know me too well,"replied the Prince. "Of course, I do." They both laughed.

At 6:30 PM, the Prince was seen leaving the Blue Clipper with Nikki. Only minutes later, they arrived at the Monte Carlo Hotel and were warmly greeted by the staff. As the couple walked through the dining room, heads turned to see His Highness and his friend escorted to their table. The Prince was stately in his white Kaftan, and Nikki quite striking in a dark blue pantsuit with a large diamond necklace. Both diners had the menu memorized and ordered quickly.

As they clinked wine glasses (the Prince's contained Perrier water as he did not consume alcohol in public), Yousif said to Nikki: "I can't tell you the details now, but soon you will earn another large commission." For the rest of the dinner, Nikki tried several ways to educe the sales information out of the Prince but to no avail.

At 8:00 the couple walked across the plaza to the casino. The Prince didn't gamble much but slowly strolled the gaming rooms, deep in thought with a smiling yacht broker on his arm. The more he surveyed the rooms, the more confident he grew that his mission would be a success.

That night, Nikki was a guest aboard the Blue Clipper III.

13

IMPLANTS

"Honey, there's a courier at the door with a package for you. Shall I sign for it?" asked Steven Goldman as he held the door open to his New York City condominium.

"Who's it from?" asked his wife, Audrey.

"All it says is HSC," replied her husband.

"OK, honey, sign for it," responded the 48 year-old Godmother of Adam Raviv.

Steven tipped the young man and closed and locked the door. Together, the couple opened the package on the pass-thru to the kitchen.

"It looks like Operation Houdini is a go," said Audrey to her husband as she unwrapped two cellphones and read the instructions in Hebrew.

"I'm to take the tour of the Federal Reserve Bank tomorrow and Friday and leave one of the cellphones at the Fed at 4:00PM on Friday afternoon," said Audrey.

"OK, honey, that means I'm in action on Saturday morning. I sure hope that Adam and his leader know what they're doing," said Steven.

"Honey, Adam is a genius. I believe he wouldn't be involved if he didn't think he could pull it off," responded his wife.

-//-

"Honey, there's a courier at the door with a package," said Jim Crowley. "Shall I sign for it?

"Who's it from," asked his wife, Ann Nichols.

"HSC," replied her husband.

Ann Nichols, age 56, retired banker and wife to Jim Crowley, Captains Crowley's brother, opened the package in their San Francisco town home.

"Honey, it's two cellphones. It means that your bother is in something really big, and I'm appointed to help. The instructions are in Urdu which I can read," said Jim.

"You're to tour the Federal Reserve Bank tomorrow and leave this cellphone there the following day at 4:00PM. I sure hope this works. I want to build that cabin in Idaho," said Jim.

"So do I," was Ann's response with real resolve in her voice.

"Good evening, Countess, your seat at the baccarat table is ready," said the Monaco Casino manager as Monika von Strassberg, the Countess of Hapsburg in Austria, arrived at the casino. This tall, muscular blond woman resembled Maria Sharapova, the tennis player. She, too, was in receipt of a package from HSC and knew exactly what to do. In the past, she had had affairs with the Prince and could be trusted.

On a cold and rainy Thursday, Audrey Goldman was in the 10:00 AM tour group at the Federal Reserve Bank on Maiden Lane in the financial district of New York City. She was bored for an hour until she was about to leave when she asked the Rent-a-Cop: "I thought we would see the computer center on the tour?"

The guard responded: "No. Since Hurricane Sandy when the basement flooded, the computer center is just above us on the second floor and not part of the tour."

"OK, I understand. The tour was great. Thank-you, Sir," replied Audrey who figured the guard's desk would be the perfect place to leave the cellphone the next day.

"This tour has been great. I thank you for your information. In fact, I'm so excited about the role of the Federal Reserve in our economy, I just may be back tomorrow," said Ann Nichols as she left the building in San Francisco's financial district.

Friday came all too soon due to the accelerated New York minute, and after her morning workout, Mrs. Goldman was back in the line for the last tour of the week at the Federal Reserve Bank. She accomplished her mission by leaving the cellphone at the guard's desk just as she was leaving the building. When she returned to her condominium, she texted: "Houdini 1 is a go."

In San Francisco, Ann Nichols smiled as she texted: "Houdini 2 is a go."

Five days later, Countess von Strassberg left the baccarat table just before the Casino closed. She had clandestinely placed her cellphone only thirty feet from the computer center. In her apartment in the wee hours of the morning, she sent a text: "Houdini 3 is a go."

Having received the messages, Adam Raviv, provided an encrypted text to His Highness: "Please set sail."

Before he went to bed, the Prince calculated the sea voyage from Cabo to San Francisco to be 31 hours and the voyage from Bermuda to New York to be 17 hours. Blue Clipper III in Monaco was already in place. Via secure satellite link, he told Dubai that Operation Houdini was a "go."

Two HSC's were underway. Adam and his two colleagues were on Blue Clipper I headed to New York.

At 8:00AM the next morning the Prince told Captain Jolie to be ready to return to Dubai in five days to remove a large cargo bound for the King Abdulaziz Hospital Center in Riyadh, Saudi Arabia.

He then made a series of phone calls. One was to Dr. St John at IBM to request technicians for the removal of the supercomputers "within six weeks." Dr. St John listened intently but in disbelief. But the Prince was a great customer and thought to himself: "He must know what he's doing."

Another call was to Win Parker alerting him of the removal of a large cargo bound for the nautical research center adjacent to the Dockyard.

A third call was made to Katie Flynn to alert her to the removal of a large cargo bound for a climate research center in Mexico City.

The Prince had trouble sleeping that night.

14

EN ROUTE

As the Blue Clipper I left Hamilton bound for New York City, the megayacht left a wake the size of two football fields. The seas were calm on this day as the huge craft was propelled along at 45 knots. Captain Crowley was on schedule to reach the mouth of the East River in fifteen and one-half hours. After a short refueling stop in Norfolk, Virginia, the HSC was off the coast of New Jersey when Catfish signaled an emergency due to a crew member with an apparent appendicitis. The New York harbormaster approved the patient drop-off at Pier 15 just below the Brooklyn Bridge on this quiet Saturday morning. The dockage window was from 9:45AM until 10:30AM.

At 9:15 that morning Steven Goldman climbed into his ambulance and headed north to the Hugh Carey tunnel leading into New York City. He proceeded to the pier where crewman were carrying a stretcher down the gangplank to the ambulance. Only a select few knew that under the blanket was a department store manikin. The ambulance turned on its siren as it left the dock and disappeared into the Financial District. At 9:55 the ambulance was silently parked at the Federal Reserve Bank at 33 Liberty Street.

On that Thursday evening, Captain Caselli was in command of Blue Clipper II as it left Cabo San Lucas for the 31 hour voyage to San Francisco. This megacraft also averaged 45 knots speed. It stopped in Long Beach, just south of Los Angeles, to refuel. Twenty-five miles west of the Golden Gate Bridge, the Captain got a secure SATCOM message to proceed with Operation Houdini.

As the megayacht passed under the bridge, Captain Caselli was granted permission to drop-off an ill crewman at Pier 3 just north of the Bay Bridge, only 5 blocks from the Financial District. He was told by the Harbormaster that ferries would start using the Pier at 10:40. The Skipper assured the authorities that the Blue Clipper would be gone by then.

At 9:20 Nathan Kalish drove his ambulance north from the City of Industry on 3rd Street right into the pier area to accept his plastic patient. Right on schedule at 9:55, the ambulance quietly parked at the Federal Reserve Bank on a foggy Saturday morning.

15

OPERATION HOUDINI

At 9:56AM, Steven Goldman got an encrypted message on his communciations consule: "Power up the cellphone." Seconds later Raviv and his team got the message that the cellphone was "alive and well." Upon seeing this message, the Blue Gene L began using the cellphone link to search for the encryption keys in the Bank's computer.

Three minutes later, Dr. Raviv confirmed: "We have by-passed the security codes and are in control of the two air-gapped computers." Less than one minute later, the SATCOM link from Monaco displayed: "Perform Operation Houdini."

The application on the supercomputer began to extract duplicate data files from the two computers. This process enabled the Deposit File on one computer and the Audit File on the other computer to each have their balances reduced by $350 million.

Twelve minutes passed, and the Blue Gene's battery pack energy level indicator signaled only three minutes of operation time left. Dr. Raviv looked at Amy and Amira and smiled as he confirmed the successful relay of the data from the ambulance to the Blue Clipper which in turn immediately relayed the data files via SATCOM to the HSBC bank in Dubai. One minute later, confirmation of the receipt of the funds was displayed on the Blue Gene and on Prince Latif's computer in Monaco. The Prince then issued a destruct command which was relayed to the ambulance, and the cellphone in the bank had its memory erased and was burned to be inoperable.

Mr. Goldman confirmed the destruction of the cellphone which was his instruction to leave the scene. He immediately proceeded to an automobile destruction facility in Perth Amboy, New Jersey. After removing the special communications boxes, he watched as a giant magnet picked up his vehicle and lowered it into a Big Daddy crusher. Five minutes later a 3,000 pound red and white cube the size of a refrigerator was lowered to the ground.

Seventeen minutes into the mission, Captain Crowley thanked the Harbormaster for his permission to drop-off his crew member.

"Skipper, you're welcome," came over the loudspeaker. "Have a safe trip to your next destination. Over." Only minutes later, the Blue Clipper I sailed past Perth Amboy and headed south out into the Atlantic Ocean.

Exactly three hours later, under the direction of Dr. Raviv, Steven Kalish received an encrypted message to power-up the cellphone in the Bank in San Francisco. Upon confirmation that the cellphone operated properly, two of Dr. Raviv's assistants aboard Blue Clipper II got the order to commence Blue Gene operations. As in New York, the supercomputer only took three minutes to bypass the security systems in the bank's computer. The extraction command was approved and the duplicate files on the air-gapped computers were found and extracted via the cellphone to the ambulance for relay to the Blue Clipper. The sum of another $350 million was transferred from the Deposit and Audit files to the Blue Gene for subsequent re-transmission to a private account in the HSBC Bank in Hong Kong.

Fifteen minutes had passed, and the Prince ordered the cellphone and the ambulance destroyed. Once Mr. Kalish had confirmed the destruction of the cellphone, he drove the ambulance to its destruction facility in South San Francisco.

Only seventeen minutes into the Operation, Captain Caselli thanked the Harbormaster for permission to dock and asked permission to resume his voyage.

"No problem, Skipper. Have a safe journey," was the response.

Once the ambulance was crushed beyond recognition, Mr. Kalish disappeared.

Upon hearing that the Blue Clipper II was headed south to Cabo, Dr. Raviv and Amy and Amira climbed aboard the Prince's helicopter for the flight to the Newark International Airport where the Prince's Gulfstream was ready to take the trio to Monaco for the final phase of Operation Houdini.

After a six-hour trans-Atlantic flight, the party landed in Nice and was driven to the Blue Clipper III in Monaco. The Prince shook the guru's hands and asked if they were ready for the next extraction.

"Yes, Your Highness, we are ready," replied the Israeli, eager to get below, down to his beloved Blue Gene.

As the Countess had confirmed the emplacement of the cellphone in the casino earlier that day, the Prince gave the command to commence the Operation once more.

It was 10:00AM on a quiet Sunday when Jacques Malreau parked his ambulance in the plaza in front of the Casino and called: "Ambulance ready."

Prince Latif in the Information & Communications Center aboard the Blue Clipper only 5 blocks away gave the command: "Operation Houdini is a "Go.""

Upon hearing this, the Frenchman used his special equipment to power-up the cellphone. Once confirmed, Dr. Raviv and the two ladies initiated Blue Gene operations. Dr. Raviv told Amy: "My guess is that we'll crack this encryption code in only two minutes."

His prediction was right. After only one minute and fifty seconds, the extraction routine began. In six minutes the target files were located and transferred via the cellphone-ambulance connection to the Blue Clipper. Dr. Raviv confirmed the receipt of $100 million in an HSBC secret account in the Bank of Scotland.

It was only then that the Prince issued the command: "Destroy the cellphone and the vehicle. Within minutes, Monsieur Malreau confirmed the destruction of the cellphone and drove away. The Prince than gave the order to shut down the supercomputer.

"Roger, Sir. We are shutting down," replied the computer guru.

Twenty minutes later, Mr. Malreau had removed the special communications suite from his vehicle, put the vehicle in neutral and with a huge grunt nudged it over a 100-foot cliff as he watched it sink to the bottom of the Mediterranean Sea.

Within the hour the giant Blue Clipper left the marina headed for Dubai as the Prince climbed aboard his Gulfstream and called Prince Khalid to report: "Operation Houdini is complete. We will commence Phase 3 of our project in five days."

16

DISCOVERY

On the following Monday at the Federal Reserve Bank in New York City, auditor Kirk Davis was reviewing the previous Friday's transactions but was unable to reconcile the deposits with the audit files.

"They are exactly $350 million different. Where did the money go? Was there a withdrawal for which I was not alerted?" he thought to himself.

"Here, please check these files," as he requested a colleague to double-check his work. He continued: "I know there is an air-gap between our primary computers, but the totals should be mirror images and both show $350 million less than the close on Friday. Something's wrong, and we need to tell the chief."

The two auditors took the elevator to the 9th floor. "Chief, Kirk has uncovered a problem. He is unable to reconcile his statements from Friday," said the auditor.

"How far is the balance apart?" asked Chief Johnnie Barnes.

"$350 million," was the reply.

"$350 million!, exclaimed the chief.

"Yes, sir, you heard me right," said Kirk's supervisor.

"Have you run the numbers a second time?" asked the chief.

"Yes, sir, with the same result," replied the supervisor.

"Looks like we need Myles on this case," said the chief as he pushed his intercom button: "Myra, please ask Ben Myles to come to my office."

As the chief continued to question the two auditors, Ben Myles entered the office.

"Hi, Boss. What's up?" asked Ben, a senior financial analyst and automation specialist.

"Ben, Ray and Kirk can't explain a variance of $350 million from Friday's close, replied Chief Barnes.

"I'm sure there is a logical explanation, boss. Do you want me to look into it?" asked Ben.

"I sure do," answered the chief. "They'll show you the findings. And I want a report as soon as possible and certainly by the end of the day."

Ben and his team met in a glass cube adjacent to the data center. Lunch was brought in as the three auditors examined the computer records. Each file was checked and double-checked for accuracy. All withdrawals were verified as authorized. Several hours passed and many search routines initialized before Myles came to the conclusion: "We're no closer to solving this when we started."

"It's 4:00PM. I'll call the chief and tell him that we're still on the case. This may be an all-nighter, guys. Better call and alert your spouses." Both auditors nodded their consent.

An hour later, the trio was reviewing the security videotapes to determine if an unauthorized person had been at the console. It was another dead end.

"Now our investigation must focus on the possibility that we were hacked from the outside," said auditor Myles. "Who knows? Maybe it was the Chinese or the Russians. They're very savvy cyber thieves, you know." said Myles.

Having satisfied themselves that the financial records had not been altered internally (although lie-detector tests were still a possibility), the team divided the task of reviewing the computer instruction code into thirds and began the painstaking process abound 8:00PM.

Around midnight and several cups of coffee later, Auditor Myles asked the team to take a break as he said: "We've found no viruses using our detection sweep. We've invoked digital forensics, complete with sandboxes. We've viewed all the network traffic since midnight on Thursday. We've found no signs of malware or extraction code, and the registry files don't appear to have been changed."

"Gentlemen, this theft, if it is a theft, requires a whole forensics team above our pay grade. Do you agree?' asked Ben Myles.

"Yes, Sir," replied Ray and Kirk.

"Ok. You guys go home and get some sleep and be ready to brief our findings in the morning," directed auditor Myles.

The two auditors closed their laptops, packed their backpacks and left the room.

Ben thought to himself: "I want to noodle this a little more before I text the chief to call in the FBI's Computer Emergency Response Team (CERT)."

Early the next morning, Ben got a call from Chief Barnes, "Ben, I read your message last night and called the FBI. They are sending a CERT team just like you requested. They should knock on your door by 10:00AM."

"Fine, chief, I'll be ready," said Ben.

Promptly at 10:00, Ben was asked to join the 4-person CERT team in a conference room. For three hours Ben explained the steps that the audit trio had taken to find the missing money. Just as the chief inspector was dismissing Ben, he got a call on his cellphone. He listened intently and an increasingly disturbed look came over his face. He asked a few questions and ended the call. As he put his phone back in its carrier, he said to the group: "It appears that the FED in San Francisco experienced the same thing. Since Friday, exactly $350 million is unaccounted for. We have a CERT team there at this very moment. Gentlemen, I'm afraid we've got an enormous heist which we must solve and quickly."

The team members looked around the table in amazement.

The chief inspector continued: "This is not the type of publicity this country needs precisely when our President is cracking down on cybercrimes. Gentlemen, let's get to work. Thank-you Mr. Myles. We'll call you if we need you. Oh, and if you come up with any additional information, please call me. Here's my card."

Auditor Myles kept asking questions to himself as he took the #7 subway train to his apartment in Long Island City. He mused that the Federal Reserve network had been compromised to extract the data. But how was it done? There was no evidence of any foul play in the network scans the team had performed. All the proper filters, encryption schemes and passwords were in place. It was a restless, almost sleepless night. About 3:00 AM, the auditor got up and fixed a cup Chamomile tea and stood at the window looking into the patio garden. The lights of Manhatten twinkled across the East River.

What kept going over and over in his mind was twofold: first, what device was used to enter the Federal Reserve's secure network, and, second, how could the encryptions codes be bypassed?

As he turned his back to the city lights, he had a revelation. "What if there were some type of listening device near the data center which could overcome the free-space air-gap between the machines. What could that be?...a cellphone maybe.

The next morning Auditor Myles called the chief of security. "Arnie, I'm conducting an investigation. Could you have the box of confiscated/lost cellphones brought to my office?"

"Yes, sir. Right away," was the chief's response. Ten minutes later Ben was sorting through about a dozen cellphones laid out on a conference table.

As he walked around the table in a reflective pose, a co-worker entered the room.

"Ben, what's up? He asked.

"I'm conducting an investigation for Chief Barnes," replied the senior auditor.

"Are you trying to decide which cellphone to buy?" joked the co-worker.

"No, not at all. I'm mulling over a concept that one of these was used in an unauthorized manner over the weekend," replied Ben.

"Oh, I see. I'll leave you to your Sherlock Holmes activity. We're still on for the Rangers hockey game on Friday, Right?" asked the FED employee.

"Sure," replied Ben as his colleague closed the door.

Wearing surgical gloves so as not to leave or smudge fingerprints, one-by-one, Ben examined each phone carefully. In many the battery was dead. Some were in bad shape as if dropped one too many times on the NYC sidewalk. He tried to make a call on several of them, but the service had been disconnected. By lunchtime, he had narrowed his search to only three remaining candidates which he carefully placed in a box with Styrofoam peanuts and placed a call to the FBI team lead.

"Sir, this is Ben Myles at the FED. I have a theory, and it's only a theory, that a cellphone was used to access our computers. I have three candidate phones. Could I ask you to run a fingerprint check on them?"

The FBI agent answered affirmatively and said, "I'll send someone over to pick them up this afternoon. It could take a day or two."

Two days later, Ben got a call from a FBI fingerprint lab technician: "Sir, all of the cellphones had been wiped clean, but in one we found two quality prints-a thumb and forefinger-on the battery. The phone itself is not functional; the circuit board overheated. I've given the prints to our database specialists. We'll see if we get a match."

Meanwhile, in Monaco, three police cars were parked in front of the Casino. Inside the building the Managing Director was briefing the detectives about the possible theft of $100 million. And in the Middle East, Blue Clipper III was nearing Dubai's Maritime City.

17

INTERPOL

In his sixth-floor office at the International Criminal Police Organization (INTERPOL) headquarters in Lyon, France, Nigel Stark, a Londoner, got a call from the Monaco police requesting help in an investigation of missing casino funds. Mr. Stark specializes in organized crime, white collar crime and, if related, computer crime.

"Detective Stark, so nice of you to take my call, and I sincerely hope you'll take my case," stated the detective on the other end of the line.

"Well, sir, I've been involved in a casino robbery before. Yes, based upon your report, it's clear that you need assistance to crack this case," replied Detective Stark. "I'll do my best."

"Detective, is this an inside job in your opinion? "You know embezzlement or theft by an employee?"

"No, Sir," came the response across the phone's speaker. "All of the employees who had access to the computer's encryption account have passed lie-detector tests," replied the detective in Monaco.

"Well, we're a worldwide organization with 800 employees representing over 100 member countries. And we have some of the best computer crime geeks on the planet. We'll do our best to get to the bottom of this. It seems similar events have just happened in the United States. The possibility of organized crime being involved has not been ruled out." said Detective Stark.

"Thank you, Detective Stark. I look forward to your findings. $100 million is a lot of money, even for our world-famous casino." finished the Monegasque as the call ended.

18

BLUE GENE GIFT I

"Captain Crowley, the containers are here for your cargo," came a sailor's voice over the intercom.

"Thank you," replied the Skipper. "I'm coming down to the cargo deck to receive them."

As the Skipper made his way down the spiral staircase, he thought to himself: "These padded containers have been in storage in Dubai and were flown here at great expense."

The next day, a group of five technicians from IBM arrived and immediately set to work dismantling the rows of connected cabinets forming the supercomputer.

"So where is this supercomputer headed now?" asked the lead IBMer.

"Ha-ha. You'll be surprised," said the salty Skipper. "Only one-half mile from here to the National Museum of Bermuda for their Nautical Research Institute to study the erosion of the reefs around the 138 islands which comprise Bermuda."

"That's a good cause," said the IBMer. "But how does a small institute afford a machine of this caliber?"

Captain Crowley replied, "It's a gift from the owner of this megayacht."

It took the five technicians a week to dismantle and pack up the sanitized Blue Gene L supercomputer for truck transport down to end of Pender Road where the museum is at Land's End.

It took another four-days for the team to dismantle the computer center, complete with the megapower modules which were donated to the city of Hamilton as back-up generators, much to the delight of the mayor. Both Captain Crowley and Dr. Raviv inspected the cargo bay to ensure there were no signs of computer power aboard the Blue Clipper I. A checklist was emailed to the Prince who then issued a sailing order: "Proceed to Monaco to Pier 16 when safe to do. May Allah be with you."

On board, only the Skipper and the guru knew it would be the last voyage of the Blue Clipper I.

19

BLUE GENE GIFT II

Captain Caselli was on the bridge if the Blue Clipper II when he was informed of the arrival of the Blue Gene shipping containers on the pier at Cabo San Lucas. The Prince's plan was executed with precision as the next day a group of IBMers arrived from California to disassemble and pack the supercomputer. The process was delayed by one day due to bad weather caused by a rare hurricane in the Pacific Ocean. But on the sixth day a convoy of five padded van trucks picked up the containers. They were headed for the Geological Institute in Mexico City. The Institute was only charged for the transportation costs as a gift from the megayacht owner.

Captain Caselli and the First Mate used the Prince's checklist to ensure there was no trace of a computer center. They were so proud of the clean-up effort, they let the Harbormaster, Katie Flynn, inspect the cavernous space. She commented: "The Prince sure has room for all of his toys down here. I can see why it was once a ferry boat."

Captain Caselli sent his checklist to the Prince who responded: "Please proceed safely to the Burrard Dry Dock Pier in Vancouver, Canada." The Skipper suspected that "HIS" Blue Clipper would be sold to a Ferry Company, but he wasn't sure. All he knew was that the four-day voyage would end with a bittersweet parting with the crew.

At the Maritime City in Dubai, the last of the Blue Gene containers were being loaded into the padded vans as the Prince and Captain Jolie looked down from the bridge.

"Your Highness," asked the Skipper, "Where is the cargo headed?"

Without taking his binoculars away from his eyes, the Prince replied: "The cargo is bound for the Prince Abdulaziz Hospital and Research Center in Riyadh, Saudi Arabia. It's a gift from Prince Khalid."

The Captain smiled his approval. He then asked: "And this ship. What will happen to it, Sir?"

The Prince was quick to reply. "Thanks to our yacht broker in Monaco, we already have several offers from royal families here in the region to keep it a megayacht."

"By the way, I've written a glowing fitness report about your professionalism, Captain. And Carnival Cruise Lines would like to talk to you about a Captain's position based out of Miami about ten miles from where your cigarette boat is docked."

A feeling of pure joy overwhelmed the Skipper.

20

ON THE TRAIL

In his conference room in Lyon, Detective Stark asked his cybersecurity team:

- How do we access a computer?
- How do we break or bypass the encryption code?
- Is a supercomputer the only machine that can do it in a short time?

What supercomputers are near the robbery sites?

- New York city- 38 miles away in Yorktown
- San Francisco-44 miles away in Livermore
- Monaco-no known supercomputers
- These machines are huge with at least 48 racks of equipment and energy hogs. How could someone hide one?
- Who makes supercomputers up to this task?"

From the audience came a resounding response: "IBM."

"OK. I agree. Where is the nearest IBM Cybersecurity Center of Excellence?"

From the audience came the answer: "Ben Gurion University in Beer Sheva, Israel."

"OK," replied Detective Stark. "Armin, you will join me in Israel next week."

"Yes, sir," was the young man's answer who has relatives in the Holy Land.

"Dr. Wetzel, you visitors are here for your 9:00AM meeting," came over the intercom.

"Thank you, Amy. Please show them into the conference room and offer coffee," said the Dean of Cybersecurity Research Center at Ben Gurion University, in part funded by IBM.

"Will do, sir."

As the two guests sipped their coffee at the conference table, a short, balding engineer with round spectacles entered the room followed by a line of young people, presumably cybersecurity "geeks."

Detective Stark and thanked his host for seeing him on short notice. "We're from INTERPOL, here is my badge, sir," as the Brit held out his hand: "I'll get right to the point. We're here to try to solve a $800 million robbery."

"How can we help you?" asked Dean Wetzel.

"Sir, it's an honor to be here where so many important cyber intrusion detection programs have been developed and are in use around the world today," responded the detective.

"Thank you, sir," replied the Dean. "We enjoy our work, and many say we're pretty good at it."

"We've had a rash of potential cyber thefts in the last two weeks, and we need to solve the case quickly, I mean very soon!" started Detective Stark. "We believe that a supercomputer may have by-passed the encryption codes of major financial institutions and stolen hundreds of millions of electronic funds without leaving a trace. In your collective wisdom, who could pull this off and how? Indeed, the funds disappeared from computers which were air-gapped. Do I make myself quite clear Dean?"

"You've come to the right place, Detective Stark," replied the Dean. "I'm sure we can help. And as you know, we have our reputation to uphold. We solve the tough ones!"

The young gurus sitting along the wall all chuckled as they knew the Dean had never let a client down in his 23 years of service to the cyber community.

"Here are my files, digital and hard copy," said the detective as he pushed a stack of large envelopes across the table.

Detective Stark then ended the meeting by saying he was only a telephone call away, and that the host governments of the United States and the Principality of Monaco needed a quick resolution of the thefts, ahead of a very curious media.

"Well, we'll do our absolute, best, sir," responded the Dean. "But this is not an exact science, and it may take longer than it is politically acceptable. If you know what I mean?"

"Sir, I perfectly understand," stated the detective. "We just need to get to the bottom of this before financial markets overreact with major sell-offs."

"Sir," said the Dean, "I fully understand the severity of the situation, and why you are sitting across from me. I will report progress as soon as I have news."

A week later Detective Stark got an email from the Institute: "Amira Atara, the guru in this banking domain, has fallen off the planet. I suggest you track her down. My guess is that she will know something about this affair."

21

MONACO

"Wellcome, Your Highness," greeted the doorman at the Hotel de Paris Monte Carlo. "Your party is already at your table."

Prince Latif glided across the marble floor of the lobby and into the mirrored dining room. Seated in the corner was Nikki Villefranche. As the Prince neared the table, she rose and slightly bowed her head as she extended her arm for a handshake. The Prince shook her hand and patted her on the back with his other hand. A warm smile came over his face. He sat down, ordered Perrier and briefly looked at the menu.

He then started the conversation: "I need your help, my dear. I have three megayachts for sale"

"What?" exclaimed the super saleswoman as her jaw dropped in disbelief.

"Your Highness," she continued. "You've only had the yachts for less than two years. They are hardly used."

Prince Latif was quick to respond, "I have no further use for them. I want them sold within 90 days. Thanks to you, I may have a buyer in the Middle East already."

"And where are they now?" Asked Nikki.

"One is in Vancouver; one is in Dubai and the third one will be here shortly," answered the Prince. "All three are in a ferry boat configuration, ready for somebody to tailor the cargo deck as desired."

"I'll pull out all of the stops, Your Highness," responded Nikki. "I'm upgrading my Dardanelle and can use the commissions."

I see," said the Prince. "And the sale price is exactly what I paid for them 18-months ago. No higher. Is that clear?"

"Yes, Sir!" replied the Prince's obedient servant. "I'll draw up the contracts this afternoon for your signature this evening if you allow me to host dinner on my boat.

"How can I refuse?" asked the Prince with a sly grin on his face.

"Perfect, then it's settled, say about 7:30," responded Nikki, also with a sly grin on her face. "Oh, and, of course, please plan to stay for dessert."

The Arab gentleman knew exactly what she meant.

22

LYON

"Detective Stark, I think I found a match in our visa database for this Atara woman you're looking for," said an analyst over the phone in his Lyon office.

"Very good, Greta, please email the dossier, directed the detective.

"Will do, sir," replied the Intern from Germany.

Moments later Detective Stark was reviewing the file on Miss Amira Atara. This Israeli woman was educated at Columbia University in New York City but was an Israeli citizen. She had earned an international reputation for keeping bank accounts secure. As she was a frequent speaker at symposiums, her passport had dozens of visa stamps.

The detective observed that her last three county visits were Bermuda, Abu Dhabi and Dubai, all major banking centers. He then sent an email to his representatives in these three countries to be on the look-out for this attractive 34-year old woman who was tall with long dark hair and resembled the actress, Natalie Portman.

That evening as Detective Stark was enjoying an Arturo Fuente Don Carlos #3 cigar and cognac, the same questions came up in his mind over and over: "How did the robbers break the 123-character encryption code, and if by computer, where is it? And if the computers at the Federal Reserve were, indeed, air-gapped, how could the files be extracted simultaneously?"

The more he thought about the crimes, the more the seasoned Sherlock Holmes realized that there was a new element to cybersecurity that had to be discovered soon, before more huge sums of money were missing.

"There must be some genius behind this, and, hopefully, if he robs again, he'll slip us, and we'll catch him."

Even after an adult beverage, sleep did not come easily that evening.

23

SCUBA

"Honey, I'm so glad we're taking this trip; I really need a break from NYC," said Audrey Goldman as she settled back into her business class seat on an El-Al flight from New York to Tel Aviv.

"I agree, honey, the timing is just right,' replied her husband, Steven. "I'm looking forward to just relaxing on the banks of the Sea of Galilee. It's been our go-to place now for twenty-years. It won't let us down this year," replied the loving husband as he reached over and stroked her on the arm.

After an uneventful flight, the couple passed through security to flag down their limousine for the trip to the northern city of Tiberias. An hour later, they unpacked in their apartment on the 7th floor of a condominium with an unobstructed view of the Sea beyond the city just below.

"Honey, let's have dinner at our favorite restaurant tonight and go scuba diving tomorrow," said Audrey.

"Sounds great to me," said her husband of 28-years.

The next morning the couple's breakfast consisted if fresh bagels, lox and cream cheese along with strong, Turkish coffee at their bistro table on the balcony.

"What a glorious day for a scuba dive," said Audrey as she put down the newspaper.

"Yes, and you know the sea so well after all the years we've been coming here," replied her husband.

"Yes, and there's a particular wreck that I've never explored. Now's my time to do so," said the New Yorker with some accent in her voice.

"Arron will take you to where you want to dive, and I'll be at the lakeside café where I think they'll name a chair after me," said Steven. "We can meet up for cocktail at Noah's Ark late in the day."

"Sounds good to me," replied Audrey as she left the balcony to gather her dive gear.

Two hours later Audrey was floating on the Sea of Galilee, just above the wreck she wanted to explore. As she spit into her mask and rubbed the spit around to help prevent fogging, she asked her friend Arron to keep the boat where it was in the water to serve as a point of reference.

"Good luck, my friend," said Arron as he lowered an anchor and watched Audrey flip over backwards to enter the water.

It was a crystal-clear day that allowed the Middle-Eastern sun to penetrate several feet below the surface.

Always the adventurer, Audrey Goldman swam down onto the deck of the sunken ship. "This is spectacular," she thought to herself. "This boat must be 1,000 years-old. It's beautiful, but a little spooky at the same time."

The experienced diver looked around the boat before entering an open hold. Her light illuminated the inside as she swam cautiously inside the hull of this ancient craft.

As she swam around, she looked at her dive watch to find she only had 5 minutes of oxygen left in her tank.

In the corner of her eye, she spotted something gleaming like a metal plate or necklace. As she reached for it, a beam was dislodged and fell on her, pinning her to the deck. She couldn't move. And the beam was over her two-way radio, so she couldn't call for help. She struggled with all might but could not free herself from this watery grave.

On the surface, Arron called her repeatedly on the radio, but there was no answer. In a panic, he jumped over and swam down about twenty-feet but saw no trace of his friend. He gasped as he got to surface and knew that Audrey would out of air at this point.

Arron called Steven and reported that Audrey was missing! Numbed by disbelief, Steven ran down to pier to meet Arron's go-fast boat. The boat sped to the spot where Steven thought he could dive to save his wife.

After twenty-five minutes and two tanks of air, Steven surfaced with the look of horror on his face. "She's gone," he cried. "She's gone!"

The next day, divers raised her lifeless body to the surface.

Arron tried to comfort his friend: "She died doing exactly what she loved."

A small ceremony was held at the family's grave as she was laid to rest within 24 hours. Steven sobbed uncontrollably through the entire event.

As he boarded his flight back to New York city, the grieving husband had no way of knowing that with his wife's death, the robbery case lead of the fingerprints on the cellphone battery was also dead.

24

CELEBRATION

In the backyard of his mansion on Al Sharq Street in the ritzy section of Dubai, Prince Latif and Dahlia were relaxing in the gazebo by the swimming pool. The Prince broke the silence: "Let's see where we're at in our Mission Houdini as he started to count with this fingers:

- The money is in three secret accounts, made extra-secure by our Israeli friends
- The sanitized Blue Gene L supercomputers are doing good things for their new owners
- In only sixty days, the Blue Clippers were sold, sans any evidence of their use on the project.
- The ambulances are destroyed or at the bottom of the sea
- The cellphones have been destroyed and should not be traced to us
- The ship's crews have dispersed around the world, and only seven of us are aware of the project, and we are sworn to secrecy
- The Bottom Line: The cost of the 3 clippers and 3 computers was $175million. We paid $45 million to outfit the ships. Fuel, operations and crew costs were$72 Million for a total expense of $292 million. And we got $92 million for sale of the clippers. In the end, it cost us $200M to have $800 million in our accounts in just two years. Not too bad. I think Prince Khalid will be pleased with the results of Operation Houdini.
- And we made a down payment on a condo in New York City."

"Dahlia" the Prince continued, "it's time to reward our team with a royal party."

"Three weeks from now, I have an important polo match. I would like them to attend as my guest, and we'll set up a tent here on the lawn for a lavish, and I mean LAVISH, party. Do you think that can be arranged?" asked the Prince.

Dahlia was quick to respond: "Yes, Your Highness, but the invitations should go out tomorrow in order to give our guests enough time to plan for the occasion."

"How many people should we plan for, Sir?"

"Sixteen to twenty," answered the Prince. "For sure the three captains, the Israelis, Nikki, Steven Goldman (what a tragedy about his wife!), the Countess, Katie Flynn, and, of course, Foster York. Aussies are always the life of the party!"

They both laughed.

"And, of course," continued the Prince, "whom ever Prince Khalid wants to invite. Let's reserve a block of rooms at the Oberoi."

"It will be done, Your Highness," replied Dahlia who was already thinking about what to wear.

The humidity was zero, but the temperature was 100 degrees the day of the polo match. The Prince's party took shelter in an air-conditioned tent sipping adult beverages while occasionally venturing out and cheering for the Prince's team. When the match ended, naturally the Prince's team won. He toweled down, changed his polo shirt and joined his guests. The focus of the conversation was about the ponies, not Operation Houdini.

At 7:30 a convoy of Maybachs brought the guests from the Oberoi to the Prince's mansion. Countess von Strassberg and Nikki Villefranche, the two Europeans, were dressed in bejeweled high fashions. Katie Flynn and Amy Grossberg looked like fashion models in low-cut, floor-length royal purple velvet gowns. Naturally, the Captains wore their evening whites. And even the Aussie trimmed his red beard for the occasion.

The celebration tent looked like an exotic movie set with ice sculptures of yachts and ponies lit up as center pieces on buffet tables. The predominant color of the evening was gold, even the silverware. Rare silk carpets were everywhere. Crystal chandeliers hung from the top of the tent. One guest was overheard saying: "It doesn't get any classier than this!"

At 8:30PM, the co-hosts asked their guests to take their assigned places at the 30-foot banquet table. Prince Khalid anchored one end and had Dahlia by his side. Prince Latif anchored the other end surrounded by Nikki, Katie and the Countess. Prince Latif rose and toasted Prince Khalid with a glass of France's finest champagne. Prince Khalid smiled and nodded his approval. The seven-course dinner was catered by the Oberoi. No morsel was left on the plates.

After dinner, the Princes circulated around the tent which had a cigar bar on one end and a cognac bar on the other end. The Skippers were seen at both ends.

At 11:30 PM, the limos arrived to take the guests back to the hotel or wherever they wished to go. Several guests continued the gala at the hotel's lobby bar until it closed.

At the mansion, the Princes met in Prince Latif's oak-paneled study to review Prince Latif's project checklist. One-by-one they reassured each other that all of the actions were completed. Prince Khalid was confident that no trace of the mission could be found.

Early the next morning, Nikki was seen in a bathrobe walking barefoot around the swimming pool while clutching a cup of coffee with both hands to her mouth. She probably felt like she was in Heaven on Earth.

25

COLD CASE

The Prince's cyber gurus, Adam, Amy and Amira, decided to remain in Dubai for three days after the celebration to shop for gold, see the sights and lounge by the hotel's pool. On one afternoon, they were treated to a "thrill ride" on Prince Khalid's cigarette speedboat. They thanked His Highness profusely, but they jointly vowed never to do it again.

Meanwhile, two INTERPOL agents convinced Detective Stark that Amira Atara was still in Dubai.

"Sir, you must station some of your people at the airport," said the Detective Stark to the local INTERPOL captain.

"As much as she travels, she will eventually have to pass through customs there. Is that clear?"

"Yes, sir," was the answer from the local authority.

The next day the three gurus arrived at the airport for their flights. With tickets and gate passes in hand, they had coffee in one of the sky lounges. Ms. Atara excused herself to go to the Duty Free Shop. As she approached the shop, she noticed two policemen asking questions to the cashier and showing her a picture. As the cyberguru turned around to leave the area, one of the policemen noticed her and commanded her to freeze in place. Ms. Atara then ran down the concourse, past a gold-platted BMW, and entered a woman's restroom. The two policemen stopped at the entrance and called for back-up.

Five minutes later, a female police officer arrived, was briefed of the situation, complete with displaying a picture of the suspect. With the area cordoned-off, the officer drew her firearm and entered the restroom. No shots were fired. It was spooky quiet. One minute later, the policewoman emerged to say: "She's dead. My guess is from cyanide."

The two policemen looked at each other and ran into the restroom, only to find the body of a woman on the floor of a lavatory stall. One of them checked for a pulse. "She's dead."

As the police were taking a body bag away from the scene, Adam and Amy passed by to catch their flight.

Back in Lyon, when the news of the death reached Detective Stark, he was heard to say: "Oh, shit! Now we really have a cold case."

26

GOLD STREET

Detective Stark resigned himself to the fact that he may retire before solving the robbery. Why?

- Only Captain Crowley knew the whole mission, and he was not a suspect. He also had a capsule just in case.)
- Adam Raviv and Amy Grossberg were not suspects, and they retired to a sequestered lifestyle behind the high walls of a city near Tel Aviv.
- Tom van der Heyden moved to a remote Indonesian island.
- Audrey Goldman was dead, and her husband, Steven, wore gloves while driving the ambulance.
- The marina managers, Katie Flynn and Win Parker were aboard a Blue Clipper but never saw the cargo bay.
- Ms. Villefranche sold the clippers but never saw the cargo bay and was able to pass lie-detector tests.
- Countess von Strassberg was above reproach.
- There were no get-away vehicles to be found.

"You know dear," the detective told his wife at the dinner table, "I may be hot on the trail of a perfect crime."

"Finish your brussels sprouts, Nigel, and get on with your life," she replied rather tersely.

A month after the celebration in Dubai, the Prince's jet landed at the JFK International Airport serving New York City. A limousine took him to his new condominium in the Financial District of

Manhatten. While in the elevator going to the 26th floor, the Prince thought to himself: "I really like this place. After all, it's on Gold Street."

As the elevator opened into his unit, a brimming Katie Flynn walked up to him and embraced her "Yousif."

For three days, the couple enjoyed New York City. They ate at fabulous restaurants, enjoyed Broadway shows and toured several art galleries. They even strolled through Central Park. The Prince rarely answered his cell phone. As the couple left the Metropolitan Museum on 5th Avenue, they hugged each other. Life was great.

At midnight of the third day, the Prince gently released himself from his lover's grasp and went to the floor to ceiling window. He looked down on the Federal Reserve Bank on Maiden Lane only two blocks from 2 Gold Street. He smiled, comforted by the flawless execution of his mission, and returned to Katie's warm embrace.

But he failed to notice the two black Suburbans that just pulled up in front of the building.

Made in the USA
Monee, IL
29 May 2023

34906141R00069